Season of Hope

BOOKS BY BRENDA S. ANDERSON

THE POTTER'S HOUSE BOOKS (TWO)

Hands of Grace
Song of Mercy
Season of Hope

THE MOSAIC COLLECTION

A Beautiful Mess
Hope is Born
Before Summer's End
Pieces of Granite
A Star Will Rise

THE POTTER'S HOUSE BOOKS

Long Way Home
Place Called Home
Home Another Way

WHERE THE HEART IS SERIES

Risking Love
Capturing Beauty
Planting Hope

COMING HOME SERIES

Pieces of Granite
Chain of Mercy
Memory Box Secrets
Hungry for Home
Coming Home – A Short Story

THE POTTER'S HOUSE BOOKS (TWO), BOOK 20

Season of Hope

A Novella

Note from the Author

The 24 books that form **The Potter's House Books Series (Two)** are linked by the theme of Hope, Redemption, and Second Chances. They are all stand-alone books and can be read in any order. Books will become progressively available from January 7, 2020.

Book 1: *The Hope We Share* by Juliette Duncan

Book 2: *Beyond the Deep* by Kristen M. Fraser

Book 3: *Honor's Reward* by Mary Manners

Book 4: *Hands of Grace* by Brenda S. Anderson

Book 5: *Always You* by Jennifer Rodewald

Book 6: *Her Cowboy Forever* by Dora Hiers

Book 7: *Changed Somehow* by Chloe Flanagan

Book 8: *Sweet Scent of Forgiveness* by Delia Latham

Book 9: *When Love Abounds* by Juliette Duncan

Book 10: *More Than This* by Kristen M. Fraser

Book 11: *Faith's Favor* by Mary Manners

Book 12: *Song of Mercy* by Brenda S. Anderson

Book 13: *In Spite of Ourselves* by Jennifer Rodewald

Book 14: *Her Christmas Cowboy* by Dora Hiers

Book 15: *Where Do They All Belong?* by Chloe Flanagan

Book 16: *Radiant Rays of Grace* by Delia Latham

Book 17: Love's Healing Touch by Juliette Duncan

Book 18: This Steadfast Heart by Kristen M. Fraser

Book 19: Hope's Promise by Mary Manners

Book 20: Season of Hope by Brenda S. Anderson

Books 21 – 24 coming soon!

Visit **www.PottersHouseBooks.com** for updates on the latest releases.

To Juliette Duncan and Becky Hrivnak ~

Thank you for welcoming me into

The Potter's House Books Series.

It's been a delight writing alongside so many gifted authors.

Truth is like the sun.

You can shut it out for a time, but it ain't goin' away.

—Elvis Presley

Chapter One

Life was good.

Veronica Whitmer—or rather Veronica Coborn now!—rolled onto her side and stared at her husband of less than forty-eight hours. He was handsome, in his geeky way, but that wasn't what had first caught her attention, the two little letters, M-D had. Call her superficial, but it hadn't taken her long to look beyond those letters.

Besides, when a woman's own father plays matchmaker with a neurologist, what's a woman to do? Say, *Sorry, I prefer the church musician?* Not likely.

Yes, life was very good, and she planned to show her appreciation with a homemade breakfast.

She softly rolled from the bed, hoping not to wake him, and tiptoed down the curved staircase to the chef's kitchen. Neither of them cooked much—that was what Iris was for. *I have a chef! And a housecleaner!* She was still trying to wrap her mind around that. Regardless, even she could throw batter into a waffle maker.

She hummed as she mixed the batter, the humming a

habit she'd picked up from her ex. Her daughter's father. With this marriage, she'd soon have the ammunition and finances she needed to get full custody of Evie. Another reason for her to rejoice today.

"You didn't wake me."

Startled, Ronnie whipped toward her husband, and her jaw dropped, muting her. Gavin the Geek was anything but. Shirtless. Tousled hair. Pajama bottoms riding low on his hips. Nearly took her breath away.

"Is something wrong?"

Oh, the man was clueless.

She regained her composure and quirked a smile. "I like your new look."

His eyes narrowed as he looked down, then he quickly crossed his arms over his body as if he hadn't just spent the past forty-plus hours as her husband. His naïveté was charming.

"Sorry." He scratched his head, tousling his hair even more. "I'll go get dressed."

"Relax, hon." She pulled out a chair and patted the back. "It's just the two of us. Let me wait on you."

"I can help."

"Yes, you can, but I want to do this for you."

He shrugged and took a seat, but his arms still barricaded his chest. It wouldn't be long before she'd have that shyness expelled.

"Where can I find the syrup?" She opened random cupboard doors, trying to familiarize herself with the space.

He began to stand. "I can—"

"Sit." She pointed a finger at his chair, and he obeyed. "Just steer me in the right direction. I need to learn my way around the kitchen, and I can't do that if you do everything for me."

"In the pantry." He sighed. "Right side, near the front, shelf at eye level."

"The pantry? You mean that walk-in-closet-sized room?" That held enough food to last through the apocalypse. Doomsday preppers would be envious.

She found the syrup exactly where Gavin said it would be, no surprise. The man had an eidetic memory on top of being a genius.

A few minutes later she set a plate filled with waffles and strawberries in front of him, and he offered to say a prayer. Though she'd grown up the daughter of a pastor, this still surprised her. Her ex had been a worship minister, and the only prayers he'd ever uttered were the melodramatic supplications in front of the congregation.

Oh, she despised phoniness.

Which was why she'd grown to love Gavin. There was nothing inauthentic about him.

She sat with her new husband, eating, enjoying the silence. With Gavin, there was no need to pollute the quiet with small talk. Another attractive attribute. Why no woman had snagged him up before now was a wonder. Apparently, prior to her, he'd shown no interest, but thanks to her father's matchmaking, she'd rescued Gavin from bachelorhood.

Her phone buzzed, intruding on their moment. She

glanced at it to see who would dare interrupt their short time alone. Mom?

Was something wrong with Evie?

"I have to take this." She grabbed her phone and swiped Answer as she walked from the room. "What's up?" She couldn't keep annoyance from her voice.

Silence. Followed by a sniffle.

Fear squeezed her veins. "Mom, what's wrong? Is Evie okay?"

Another sniffle, and a cough. "She's fine." Her voice came out mousy. "I can't talk about it. Come get Evie, and come alone."

What? She wasn't making any sense. "I don't under—"

The phone clicked, ending the call. Ronnie stood in the living room, staring at the screen, shivering.

"What's wrong?" Gavin's warm hand rested on her shoulder.

"I…" She looked up into his grey eyes and slowly shook her head. "I don't know. It's the weirdest call ever. She wants me to pick up Evie. Now. Alone."

"Then that's what you do." Always matter of fact, no reading between the lines. "I'll clean up breakfast." Oh, the man was a gem.

"Thank you." She stretched up on her tippy toes to kiss him. "I love you."

"And I love you." Simply said, but coming from him, she knew his words were genuine.

She threw on a pair of jogging pants, a long T-shirt, and some flip-flops, and hurried to her Prius. After backing onto the street, she tried flooring it, but the stupid thing had no get-up-and-go. Right now, saving the planet with a car mattered a whole lot less than it used to. She'd give anything for a muscle car.

Still, she broke all the speed limits driving to her parents' place. If Evie was okay, what was wrong with Mom? It had to be her dad, and that thought made her feel like vomiting. As an only child, her father doted on her. In her eyes, no one measured up to him. Definitely not her ex. Gavin? Not yet—she'd only known him for two years—but he was the first man she'd met who came remotely close.

Twenty long minutes later, she turned onto her parents' street and slammed on her brakes. Cars clogged the road. News vans, too. And people wielding microphones crammed the end of the driveway.

What in the world?

Should she call Mom back and ask what was going on? Oh, if only Gavin were with her, he'd know what to do and could run interference.

She hit the Call button on her steering wheel. The phone rang on and on without an answer. Which meant Ronnie needed to push on through whatever this was. Was Mom okay? Dad? Evie? And how would any of that involve the news?

Slowly, she inched forward, and the masses parted, but then they crowded her car, ramming their microphones in her direction, shouting unintelligible things.

The gurgle in her gut warned her that whatever this was about was life-changing, and she needed to remove Evie from the situation.

Ignoring the reporters, she pressed through the crowds and finally squeezed up on the driveway of her parents' modest home. A small rambler that didn't brag about her father's success as the head pastor at a megachurch. He took the Bible's call to humility to heart.

With reporters shouting things that made no sense, she let herself in the side door, closed it, then leaned against it, breathing hard as if she'd just escaped with her life from a pride of lions.

Once her breaths evened, she surveyed the home she could see from the door. Mom wasn't in the kitchen or the living room.

Would she be downstairs or in her bedroom? Bedroom first.

Ronnie hustled through the living room, grateful that the drapes were closed to the mob outside.

She braked to a stop outside the bedroom door. Why were Mom's clothes laid out on the bed?

And where was she?

More importantly, where was Evie?

Take a deep breath, Ronnie.

They were likely playing downstairs, away from the outside chaos. She slowed her pace to the steps and gave herself a pep talk going down. Everything was okay. What was going on outside had a reasonable explanation. Evie was fine. Dad was fine. Life was good, right?

She reached the bottom of the steps. Toys littered the family room, but Evie wasn't there, which meant she and

Mom were in the back room where Evie's crib was. This early in the morning, Evie wouldn't be taking a nap, but the house was eerily silent. Ronnie approached the closed bedroom door with her nerves zinging, afraid to learn what was behind it.

She knocked. Waited. Let herself in.

Straight ahead, Evie lay in the crib, sucking her thumb, her eyes closed. Her cheeks were wet from tears.

And on the twin bed lay Mom. Curled in the fetal position, an open suitcase at her feet.

"What's going on?" The words tumbled from Ronnie's brain and whispered from her mouth. None of the pieces of this puzzle fit together.

Mom sniffled as she slowly sat up and draped her legs over the side of the bed, her gaze glued to the carpeted floor. "It's your father."

No, no, no. Was that what the reporters were here about? Had something happened to Dad? Her legs became like rubber. He had to be okay.

But that idea didn't mesh with what Ronnie saw in the house.

Mom's clothes on the bed.

The suitcase.

On trembling legs, Ronnie moved across the room then sat beside her mom, who was radiating a don't-you-dare-hug-me vibe.

Ronnie steeled her nerves and her voice. "What about Dad? And what's with the suitcase?"

Mom laughed, shaking her head. "Oh, he's done it now."

Done what? What would he do that would involve the press?

Ronnie remained silent, hoping her mom would want to fill the quiet. Dad was a good man. Loved by his church.

And Mom.

At least he used to be.

"I can't live with the fool one second more."

Whoa. That was Dad she was calling a fool. Ronnie couldn't stay silent. "What did you do? Chase him away?" That wouldn't be newsworthy, but that was all Ronnie could think of.

"Oh, that's rich." Mom wiped a hand over her nose. "I did nothing. It was all your father."

No longer able to contain herself, Ronnie leaped up and glared down at her mom. "Why are reporters stalking our home? What. Happened?"

Evie began whimpering, so Ronnie retrieved her from the crib, bounced her on her hip.

Mom looked up, a lifeless stare in her eyes that made Ronnie's blood freeze as if winter raged outside.

"That man you adore." Mom spat out the word. "That man who can do no wrong in your eyes or the congregants' eyes. He's gotten himself arrested."

Chapter Two

In spite of the ninety-plus degree temperatures outside, Ronnie began shivering.

"No." She shook her head, cuddling Evie as close as possible to her body. "Whatever it is he's accused of, it's wrong."

"I take it you haven't watched any news." Mom suddenly got this arrogant confidence, as if she were gleeful about her husband's arrest.

"Of course not. We've been, uh..." This was not the conversation to have with her mother. "We haven't been married for two full days even. What do you think we've been doing?"

Not even a blush from her mom.

"Just tell me what's going on." Ronnie stroked the back of Evie's head to keep her calm. No doubt she felt the tension pulsing in this little room.

Mom stood and stared out the egress window toward the street. "You're aware of the vandalism done to Kyle's home."

Kyle. Her ex. She gritted her teeth. She nodded then

realized her mom's back was to her. "Yes, I am. Sounds like his dad deserved it."

"He was innocent."

"How do you know? Because Kyle's ex-girlfriend says so?"

"Because the police said so."

Oh.

Fine then. "Still, it's no surprise someone would graffiti the house of a child stalker, even if he was innocent." Even she knew that argument was lame, but it kept her from hearing the accusation against her own father.

Mom whipped around and glared at Ronnie. "Those vandals were paid off by your father."

Ronnie blinked. "What?" She shook her head and paced as Evie's whimpering grew stronger. No way. It couldn't be true. "That's a lie."

"Is it?" Mom's eyes softened. "I know you adore him. I did once as well."

"Once?"

"Until his ego outgrew the ministry."

"Uh-uh. True North loves him."

"They love his persona. They love that he tells them what they want to hear, just as he's always told you what you crave to hear from him."

"What I crave to hear is that he's innocent. The vandals...did they accuse him?"

"Sit, Ronnie." Mom sat on the bed and patted the space beside her.

Ronnie kept Evie in her arms, not to soothe the toddler,

but to calm herself. "Just tell me."

Mom, the woman who had always looked so strong to Ronnie, suddenly appeared frail. Old even. "Yes, the vandals accused him. Once they were caught, they sang louder than the worship band at True North."

A little dig at the band wasn't uncommon for Mom. She'd never appreciated the contemporary sound.

"Fine. They accused Dad, that doesn't mean he paid them."

"He admitted it, Ronnie."

Her arms shook with the shivers, and Evie wailed. Ronnie brought her to the crib and laid her down which brought on louder cries.

At the moment, Ronnie didn't care. Her world was crashing around her, and she wanted to wail just like her daughter. She stomped from the bedroom to get away from Evie and the lies her mom had to be telling. Dad would never do such a thing. He was good. Kind. He was a pastor, for goodness' sake.

"I'm sorry, Veronica."

She felt her mother at her side, taking her hand, leading her to the couch, making her sit.

"I'm so sorry, darling." Mom sat beside her, stroked her hair like when she had been a child.

"Is he..." She whispered. "Is he in jail?"

"He is."

"Bail?"

"Dick from True North is posting. I refused."

"How?" She jerked her head toward her mom. "You'd let

him sit in jail?"

"For putting you and me and Kyle and his father through this? You bet I would. His ego has grown too big."

Made no sense. He wasn't arrogant. He was her father, who loved her. Would do anything for her.

Anything…

Oh no.

Tears threatened, but she rebuffed them. "He didn't do this for me, did he?"

"You wanted full custody of Evie."

She hugged herself. "Not this way." She looked toward the bedroom, where Evie screamed. *I feel the same way, Evelyn. I really do.*

"There's more."

More? Phlegm already coated her throat. Ronnie couldn't stomach any more.

"It's about Gavin."

No. Not Gavin. The man was perfection. She hugged herself, steeling herself against her mom's words.

"Your father set you two up with the express purpose of breaking up you and Kyle."

Ronnie's hands fidgeted. She knew that about her father and Gavin. Her husband had told her early on that Dad had played matchmaker before Gavin knew about Kyle. By the time he found out about Kyle, she'd made the decision to break up with him. With Kyle there had been no future. They had been two people living together, moving in separate directions.

Evie's wails sent a shiver up her spine.

When Gavin initially proposed, neither of them knew she was pregnant with Kyle's daughter. By then, reconciliation with her ex was out of the question.

"Once Dad made the introduction, he stepped out of the way." She held up her chin.

"Did he?"

"Of course, he did."

"Then why the sudden wedding Sunday afternoon? What happened to your big wedding plans?"

"Because…" Because Gavin brought up the fact that if she wanted full custody of Evie, being married would play in her favor. "It was Gavin's idea."

"Was it?"

"Of course it was." Evie's cries became insistent. Oh, she was a bad mom, but she had to get the truth out, and she couldn't do that if Evie was clinging to her.

Mom pinned her to the sofa with her intense gaze. "Are you certain the abrupt wedding was Gavin's idea?"

No, she wasn't. She shrunk down, no longer having the strength to hold up her shoulders. "Doesn't matter anymore, does it?"

"You're married, so the damage is done."

Damage? Her mom was talking nonsense. Still, the thought of Gavin being her father's puppet, of him doing things just to appease her father, niggled at her

"Then suit yourself." Mom stood. "Just don't overlook the possibility that the vandals weren't the only ones your father recruited."

"What are you saying?"

"Ask your new husband what was in it for him with your marriage? Ask him about that empty seat on the church board."

Church board seat? Sure, Gavin had expressed interest, seeing the need for some changes in the church, but...but what? She couldn't wrap her brain around the idea of Gavin and her dad using her as a pawn. They loved her. They wouldn't do that.

Would they?

Oh, now Mom had her doubting everything she knew to be true.

"Ignore me." Mom waved her hand. "Right now, I'm angry with the world, and everyone's guilty."

Everyone? "Me too?"

Mom opened her mouth then clamped it shut. "I can't trust anything I say right now to be kind, so we'll leave it at that. If you need me, I'll be staying at Grandma Eva's."

Something in Ronnie's brain clicked. The clothes. The suitcase. "You're breaking up with Dad?"

"Sweetheart, he did the breaking up long ago. It's time I finally recognized it." She aimed for the back room. "Get your daughter and go home to your husband. See if your marriage is worth saving. Any marriage begun on faulty premises is doomed to fail. Even if that failure is forty years down the road, like mine."

Reporters clogged the road to Gavin's—no, *her* driveway to the spacious home. She'd managed to evade them at Mom and Dad's, and believed she'd escaped, but now this.

Thankfully, Evie had slept all the way home, having cried herself out at Nana and Papa's.

Nana and Papa's...

She managed to squeeze between the press and took her time driving up the long, curvy driveway to the home. She parked in the garage, then lay her head against the rest and closed her eyes. Her parents couldn't break up. Her dad couldn't be guilty of such a horrible crime.

Then there was Gavin. Had he been in cahoots with her father? Her relationship with Gavin was what had ultimately ended her relationship with Kyle. This marriage made getting full custody a possibility.

Was she clueless for not seeing anything nefarious in Gavin's sudden desire to move up their wedding? Or had Mom planted weed-filled ideas in her head?

What she'd give to go to bed, so when she'd awaken, all this would just be a nightmare, not reality. She'd be deliriously happy with her new marriage and her new home.

Maybe that last part was still her reality.

She forced herself to step out of the car and retrieve an exhausted Evie from the back seat. She kissed away the salty remnants of tears.

"I'm sorry, baby girl."

Evie snuggled against her shoulder. Secure. Just as Ronnie had always felt with her father.

Had that security all been a lie?

Where...why...when had he gone off the rails?

The door to the house flung open, and Gavin stood beneath the frame, changed from this morning. Black framed glasses. Hair combed like a dad from some 1950s sitcom. Polo shirt and pleated shorts. A hundred percent geek, and she loved him.

But was that enough?

Had he been conspiring with her dad all along? The insinuation by her mom couldn't be ignored.

He came around his Mercedes and stopped short of hugging her. Reading body language wasn't his forte, so he tended to stand back until she invited him into her space.

"I've heard the news about your father. I'm sorry, Veronica."

Not as much as she was. She just nodded her acknowledgment.

His gaze flitted to Evie then back to Ronnie. "Is she all right?" He'd always loved Evie as if she were his own. And by the way Gavin pinned his arms to his side, Ronnie could tell that he longed to hold his stepdaughter. That was a good sign, right?

"She's fine." Ronnie gratefully handed her over, and Evie immediately snuggled in his arms. The same way Ronnie had always found comfort with her father. "Just cried out." She nodded to the door to the house. "Let's go in and talk."

Not that she really wanted to talk things out today. She was already exhausted, but her fairytale life had been ripped out from beneath her, and she needed to know the truth, whatever that was.

They stepped into the house, and Gavin lowered Evie to the floor. She eagerly took his finger and walked beside him. That was trust. He'd better not break that trust, or it would break her daughter's heart. That was an unforgivable offense.

Gavin led the way to the playroom, if that was what you wanted to call it. Shelves lined with toys framed in two walls, and comfy adult seating circled the middle. Evie toddled right over to a toy basket and began unloading it. That would keep her occupied for several minutes.

He sat on the loveseat and patted the space beside him, but she needed to see him head-on when he gave his answers.

"How are you doing?" He leaned toward her, for him a practiced body language.

How was she doing? She looked out the window at a manicured garden. "I don't know. I'm angry. Confused. Unbelieving. Exhausted."

"Understandable. And your mom?"

Ronnie shook her head, still trying to wrap her brain around this. "She's moving out. Going to stay with Grandma Eva." Evelyn was named after her, but Ronnie refused to saddle her daughter with the name Evangeline.

"Temporary?"

"I hope so."

"Maybe this is what your mom and dad need to grow closer together."

She laughed sarcastically at that. "Sure, breaking them

apart is a great way to mend a relationship."

"How—"

"Uh-uh. It's my turn. I have questions for you."

He squirmed at that. A sign of guilt?

"I know Dad set us up, but what I don't know is if it was his idea or yours."

His brows raised, and he sat back. Did creating distance between himself and the question communicate remorse or innocence?

"His. Not that I hadn't noticed you." He smiled at that. "But I thought you were taken. Which apparently you were."

It was her turn to squirm.

"When he recommended asking you out, I took the chance. When you said *yes*, I assumed you were available."

She looked down at her fidgeting hands. Sure, make it all about her mistakes. She had to turn it back on him.

"You and Dad were close." She raised her chin, regaining control of the conversation. "Did you know anything about the vandals he hired?"

"*Allegedly* hired."

Avoiding the answer. Definitely an indication of guilt, and that made her want to heave. "Not according to Mom. She's already convicted him." Like mother, like daughter.

He splayed his hands. "Can you blame her? The man she lived with for over forty years isn't the man she thought he was."

Are you the man I think you are? She caught herself staring and shook her head.

"Let me get to the point." She leaned toward him, but he didn't back away. "Whose idea was it for you to rush the wedding to this past Sunday?"

He looked down, and that made her want to throw something.

"Your father—"

"Please look me in the eye." She needed to see his expression, as neutral as he could be, she'd learned to read him over the past couple years.

He looked up, their gazes met, and he gulped. "He'd brought up how Kyle's home was unsuitable for Evie, with people tagging the house. I couldn't disagree. And then he…he didn't make the suggestion outright…he commented how full custody for you…us…was more likely to occur if we were married."

"Wow…" She watched Evie turn the pages in a book and read it with a language all her own.

If that was all Dad and Gavin had conspired, she could live with it, but the answer to her next question could determine the fate of their very short marriage.

"Did Dad offer you a seat on the church board in exchange for marrying me?"

His eyes bugged out, amplified by his eyeglasses, and his mouth hung open.

Shock at the absurdity of the question or at her knowing about her dad's offer?

"I…" He turned and looked at Evie, so content and surrounded by toys.

Toys didn't betray you. Like dads and moms did.

Like husbands did.

Gavin's avoidance of her question made her want to cry.

"Well?" Her fingers clenched together as if in prayer, but that was the only thing that kept her from throwing something at her "husband."

He finally turned toward her, but his eyes completely avoided hers. His hands were folded together as well, but in a wringing posture. Trying to wrangle his way out of the situation? Free himself from his lies? His collusion with her father, the crook?

"He did." So, the man could speak. "But—"

"Uh-uh." Her hands broke free and clenched in fists. "So, our marriage had nothing to do with love."

He blinked rapidly. What that meant, she had no idea.

"You know I love you," he finally said, his hands splayed.

Did she? Not anymore. "Is love enough? Why is it, the only times you make a move is when my dad pulls your strings?"

His eyes narrowed and anger darkened them. "Don't go places you can't find your way out of."

"That's not a denial."

He sighed loudly and brushed both hands through his once-neat hair. "This is exactly why I avoided relationships."

He did not just say that. Her heart began palpitating, and she pushed off the chair to retrieve Evie. "Time to go home, baby girl." She held the lease on her apartment for another six months, until the new year. With the sudden marriage, all her belongings were there yet as well. They'd planned to sublet the place. Well, not anymore. She swooped up her daughter, and the plastic truck she held crashed to the floor.

"I'm sorry. That was wrong of me to say." His voice was low and tremulous behind her. "You're already home."

She turned to face him, using Evie as a shield between them. "Am I? Whose truth is that? Am I only your wife because Dad was pulling your strings? I can't help but wonder if you were involved with the vandalism, too."

"I had nothing to do with the graffiti."

"But you didn't deny anything else." She held Evie tightly. "I can't...I need time alone to figure things out. Nothing—nobody's who I thought they were."

He sighed again. "Fine. I'll give you privacy, but you and Evie stay here. I'll leave."

"I can't let you do that. This is your house."

He stepped close to her, invading her space. "This is *our* home. Now and whenever you get things figured out. Just know that I do love you, fiercely. I love Evie as if she were my own blood, and I will do whatever it takes to keep us together. Even if that means letting you go."

There he went again, speaking nonsense.

"I'll find a place to stay close to the clinic." He reached over and touched her cheek.

She shrunk back as if slapped. "I can't stay here. I'm going back to my apartment."

His eyes closed and he slowly nodded. From experience, he knew better than to argue with her.

"I'll pack Evie's things." He turned from her.

"No." She needed to do this on her own. Any more time around Gavin, and she might just cave in. Who knew he was a great actor along with being a brilliant neurologist?

"I'll be ready whenever you are, and I'll be praying for you every moment."

Rather than reply, she hurried from the room, outside where she could put Evie down and let her run. Where Ronnie could hide from the world that had lied to her. She glanced upward at skies feathered with clouds. Angel wings?

Gavin was praying for her...were the wings an answer to prayer?

She was a PK, a preacher's kid, and yet she knew nothing about God. Not really. Just that He was a fun stealer, and she'd spent much of her youth and adulthood trying to prove that she didn't need Him.

Guess Dad and Mom and Gavin had solidified that idea. Besides, if a preacher couldn't be obedient, how could anyone else be expected to behave?

Chapter Three

onnie remained outside, calming herself. She was acting like a diva, but how are you supposed to react when your life has been turned upside down and inside out?

She should have allowed Gavin to gather Evie's things, then she wouldn't have to go back inside the dream home she was leaving behind.

Forever? Today, that was what the knots in her stomach were communicating.

She heard a door close behind her and braced herself in case Gavin pleaded with her to stay.

"Evie's diaper bag."

He wasn't going to beg for her to stay? Why did that hurt worse?

She didn't want to face him, but she was an adult, she could behave like an adult, right? She steeled her expression and turned toward him.

As if extending an olive branch, he held out the diaper bag, a Vera Wong bag that looked like a purse. Another lie.

"Thank you." Accepting the bag, she kept her face

expressionless. She hoped, anyway. Then turned away from him and called Evie. "Time to go home, sweetie."

Gavin sighed behind her. She didn't care—rather, she refused to show him that she did.

The pouting child trudged toward Ronnie on little legs that normally zoomed faster that the Energizer Bunny. She'd grown to love Gavin's place. What child wouldn't? An acre of land to run on as opposed to the tiny apartment playground that was too often occupied with older kids messing around.

Kyle's little place would have more room.

Kyle...

That was what she'd do.

She hurried to her daughter and scooped up the squirming girl. "Would you like to go see Dada?"

Just like that, Evie's pout-filled countenance lifted into a sunshine-filled face. This child was so fortunate to have two fathers who loved her, even if Ronnie wasn't happy with either of them. Both would do anything for Evie.

Ronnie strode toward the house, swinging wide of Gavin.

"You're bringing her to Kyle's?"

She looked to her right to examine his expression. Was he upset by Evie going to her father's place? His poker face told her nothing.

Taking command of the conversation, she raised her chin. "Is that a problem?"

He shook his head. "I think that's a good idea."

As if she cared what Gavin thought right now.

"At least let me say goodbye to Evelyn."

She puffed out a breath. "Fine."

He closed the gap she'd intentionally placed between them, close enough to kiss Evie on the cheek. Close enough for his presence to invade her space without them touching.

"I'll miss you, Jelly Bean." He bopped her nose, and she giggled. "See you soon."

He looked directly at Ronnie for those last three words as if expecting her to say something in return.

Not likely.

Instead she hurried from the backyard, through the gate, to her car waiting in the open garage. She backed down the driveway, parted the media who still hung around, and squealed onto the city street before she could change her mind.

Was she making the worst mistake of her life? Leaving behind a new husband and his elaborate home because she'd been a pawn in her father's and husband's schemes?

No, she had to do this. As her mom had said, a marriage built on a faulty premise would eventually fail, so she may as well end it now rather than waste years of her life as Mom had.

But had Mom's years together with Dad really been wasted?

Ugh. Her entire world was grey, when what she wished for was black and white, a world where everyone didn't have their own truths.

Tomorrow, she'd go into work where she dealt with numbers all day. One plus one always equaled two. She liked the reliability of that.

Today, she had to face her ex.

She shivered at the thought. Not because he'd do anything bad to her, but he'd probably be syrupy nice, and she'd once again regret her decision to break up with him.

For Gavin.

Wow. That had sure worked out well.

She pounded the steering wheel, angry at herself for being so stupid. For being thrilled at the notion of a quick wedding. Now she was stuck.

Or was she?

She turned on the car radio and found a local Christian music station, one Kyle would have listened to. Her fingers tapped to the beat, just as Kyle's always had, but he usually sang along.

Would he take her back?

Don't go there, Ronnie. Math told her that one mistake plus another—rather two plus one more—equaled three mistakes. One didn't subtract from the other.

So, what was the right thing to do?

She looked in the rearview mirror at Evie. The right thing to do was what was best for her child. What that was, though, Ronnie had no clue. Not with her brain a pile of mush and her heart broken worse than Humpty Dumpty.

Kyle's place was a world away from here, on the opposite end of the Twin Cities. A good hour's drive. To erase everything from her mind, she sang along with the radio, trying to digest what the lyrics were saying. Something about our hope being in God. That was what Dad had preached.

Guess he didn't live out his own sermons.

Too soon, she was driving down the street toward Kyle's home, half of a duplex owned by his father. The ugly words that had been painted across the front a few weeks back were hidden by a layer or two of fresh paint. An unfamiliar car sat in the driveway. Did he have company?

Didn't matter. She needed to drop Evie off so she could go home and make sense of her life.

"Let's go see Dada." She extricated Evie from the car seat and carried her to Kyle's front door.

She held her breath. Knocked. Waited.

The door flung open.

Kyle's brows shot up. "Ronnie?"

"Dada!"

He blinked, but that didn't hide the tears glossing his eyes as daughter reached for father. "Hey, baby girl, Dada's missed you so much." Closing his eyes, he dug his nose into what little hair Evie had.

A scorched scent struck Ronnie's nostrils. "Something's burning."

Surprise lit his face again and he handed Evie back. "Here."

She followed him into the home and watched him mutter something over burnt toasted sandwiches. The peanut butter and banana sandwiches had long been a favorite of his. After what her father had put Kyle through, no wonder he made the comfort food.

"Sorry about that." She glanced around the sparsely furnished room, checking the outlets for covers, kitchen cabinets for locks. It looked good, but…"Is it childproofed?"

"It's safe," he grunted back, clearly irritated with her question, but when it came to her daughter, she was going to be fiercely protective.

"Good." She lowered Evie to the ground, and the child toddled toward the corner of the room where a bright red crate sat with a bunch of toys. "I need to talk to you."

"It can't wait? It's been a long couple of days."

"I know." She sniffled. Now she felt like crying? In front of Kyle? She dabbed at her eyes.

"I'm sorry. That was rude." He nodded toward the couch that looked like he'd rescued it from a secondhand store. But it appeared to be clean, so she sat beside him.

"How are you doing?" he asked. "How's your mom?"

"How do you think we're doing?" She wiped her wayward tears again. "The man I've looked up to all my life suddenly becomes a…a criminal? I can't wrap my head around it."

"If it helps any, he was doing it for you, wanting the best for Evie, and that wasn't me apparently."

Apparently not.

If Dad hadn't intervened, would she still be with Kyle? Would their little family be intact yet?

"Did you know Dad introduced me to Gavin?"

Kyle nodded.

"I love him." I think. "He's a good man," she said, more to convince herself. "But this mess, it taints everything."

Kyle sat silently, probably in agreement. More tears threatened, which meant it was time to leave. Once she got home, then she'd allow herself a good cry, but not now, not in front of him.

She wiped her eyes and sat up straight. "Are you okay to take Evie now? Gavin and I, we need to work some things out."

"Of course."

"Thank you." She stood and looked to the corner at the daughter she and Kyle had created together. Even with all the bad choices they'd made, Evie was still a blessing. How could something beautiful come out of a broken relationship?

She looked to the man she'd hurt two years back with her double announcement that she was pregnant with his child and that she was leaving him for another man. At that time, it had seemed so logical. Now...

Now was time to swallow a little bit of her pride. "You're a good man, Kyle Stevens."

He looked to the floor. "I wish I'd been better for you."

She laughed sarcastically. "That makes two of us." She opened her arms, needing a hug, even it if was from Kyle, one that communicated both "I'm sorry" and "Goodbye."

Then she released him. "I'll see you in a week?"

He nodded.

Hopefully by then she'd have her head screwed on straight, and life would start to look normal again. Well, as normal as it could be going forward.

"Evie, honey, come say bye-bye to Momma."

Their daughter remained by the toy bin. Didn't look back. Just waved.

Her own daughter was dissing her. "See how I rank." Her

lips pinched together, preventing that onset of tears. "Take good care of her."

She stalked out the door.

Empty handed.

In a matter of a few short hours, her life had gone from overflowing with goodness to bottom-of-the-barrel dry.

At least now she could go home, to her apartment vacant of anyone but her, and have a good cry.

Chapter Four

A song blaring from Ronnie's phone woke her. Couldn't be morning already, could it? She swiped the *Dismiss* button to shut off the alarm then looked at the time. Six AM.

How could that be when she'd laid down at seven PM the night before to have a good cry all by herself?

But she hadn't cried. She'd lain there, emotionally exhausted.

Still was. She hugged a pillow to her chest and rocked. The last thing she wanted to do was go in to work today and face the marriage and family therapist she worked for. Hannah would spot Ronnie's misery before they were in a room together. She was that good.

But Ronnie had to work. Especially now. The child support she received from Kyle was only a drop of what she needed to maintain her lifestyle—the lifestyle she'd gotten used to while dating Gavin.

Oh, she was a fool!

But she wasn't foolish enough to wallow at home.

The best way to feel good when life surrounding you was

stormy was to fool the mirror. Do her makeup. Dress in her best go-to-work outfit. Looking good always helped. And without Evie here to interrupt...

Oh, Evie...

Just like that, a rain cloud shrouded her. Was her daughter going to grow up with two dads who loved her yet didn't live with her? Hannah would say that was the perfect recipe to whip up a mental and emotional mess.

Feeling sorry for herself would only add sour flavor to that mess.

"You can do this, Veronica," she told the woman in the mirror, quoting an oft-used phrase by Gavin. That was love, wasn't it?

"Move on, girl!" Her legs obeyed, transporting her to the Prius. Again, she let the radio music take the space where pity wanted to reside.

A few minutes later, she strode into the small office she was in charge of. Just her and Hannah. Hannah counselled the sick while Ronnie did everything else. Answer phones, schedule appointments, keep the plants alive, do bookwork, troubleshoot computer problems. She loved the variety of work. And she appreciated that it was all straightforward. Her duties were laid out with no subjectivity.

On her side of Hannah's office door, everything was black and white. Two plus one equaled three.

Hannah's side was a mess, yet somehow Hannah always— or most often—managed to sweep that mess into beauty.

Ronnie wrote out on sticky notes Hannah's

appointments for the day. That way, when one task was completed, Hannah would recycle that note and move on to the next task or appointment. That helped keep her organized in the midst of chaos.

Moments after Ronnie finished jotting down the schedule, Hannah walked in. She stopped abruptly and squinted at Ronnie.

"Uh-oh."

"Uh-oh?" Ronnie looked around the room for something amiss, but everything was in its rightful place. "What's wrong?"

"What time is my first appointment?"

The counselor answering a question with another question was never a good sign.

Ronnie glanced at the top sticky note. "Thirty minutes."

"Good. Just enough time." She nodded toward her door. "Come on in."

"Uh-oh."

Hannah grinned and held the door for Ronnie, then closed it behind her.

Uh-oh was right. A closed door meant a conversation was about to happen that no one else should hear.

As much as she didn't want to, she sat in the comfy chair usually occupied by patients. Though the chair felt a bit prickly today.

Instead of sitting by her desk, Hannah set her chair directly in front of Ronnie. She looked into Ronnie's eyes in a way that made her feel bare.

Ronnie crossed arms over her chest and looked away, though Hannah would likely read that action as avoidance.

Which was true. "You saw the news."

"I'm so sorry, Ronnie."

"Yeah. Me too." She looked upward, still avoiding Hannah's gaze. "But you don't know the rest of the story."

"I figured so. This is always the outfit you choose when life hands you lemons."

"Seriously?" She was that transparent?

Hannah just smiled. "Want to talk about it?"

Her boss—and friend—was the only one Ronnie would talk to. Right now, the only person she trusted.

"I got married on Friday."

Hannah blinked. Uh-hah, Ronnie even surprised her.

"And yesterday, I left Gavin."

"Oh, my."

"Is that the best you have, counselor?"

"That's the best your friend has. Would you prefer I shift into counselor mode?"

Ronnie shook her head. A friend was far more valuable. She proceeded to relay the conversations with her mother, with Gavin, and even Kyle.

"Besides you, I don't know who I can trust anymore."

"Have you tried praying?"

Hannah was always more spiritual than Ronnie, and patients came to her for that very reason.

"In case you didn't notice, the man who taught me about God, the person who first showed me how to pray, is in jail. Or at least he was yesterday. No clue if he's out on bail yet. To be honest, I don't want to know when he gets out."

"You're justifiably angry."

"Yes, yes I am, and that's about the only truth I know."

Hannah shifted. Cocked her head. A tell from her. She was about to impart some wisdom that would make the storm clouds recede, or she'd say something that would make the storms angrier yet.

"I have an assignment for you."

"Naturally." Ronnie didn't even resist rolling her eyes.

"Oh, you do that well."

"Thanks?"

Hannah laughed then quickly sobered. "I get it. Life has thrown a royal fit your way, and through the murkiness it's difficult to discern the truth."

"Do you talk like that to all your patients?"

"Are you trying to avoid my assignment?"

"There you go again, answering a question with a question."

"It's a hard habit to break." Hannah smiled then leaned forward. "I want you to learn what truth is."

"Huh?" She looked around the room and spotted the book she wanted. A Merriam-Webster dictionary. She retrieved it and opened it up to the T's. Read the first definition, "The body of real things, events, and facts."

"Okay. Now take that definition and apply it to those around you."

"Well, that's easy. My dad's a hypo—"

"It's important to remove emotion from what you find."

"That doesn't change what my dad is."

"Doesn't it?"

"Would you stop that?" Ronnie stood and glared down at her friend. She'd been right—what Hannah had to say would make her angrier yet. And her friend just sat there, silently, unconcerned by Ronnie's outburst.

Ronnie sat back down, slumping in her chair. "How do you do it?"

"It's magic." She wiggled her eyebrows. "But seriously, I've seen this brewing on your horizon for a while now. It's a good thing for you to explore."

"Just how do I do that?" She held up the dictionary. "If you won't allow this?"

Hannah wagged her finger. "I didn't say that wasn't allowed. I said apply that definition to those around you. To events around you. I want you to explore what is truth."

"And if I don't come up with the answer you're looking for?"

"I'm not looking for a specific answer."

"So, truth is subjective?"

"Is it?"

Ronnie just shook her head. "You're exasperating."

"Why, thank you." Hannah got up and gestured toward the door.

Ronnie resisted sticking out her tongue at her friend. Her free session was up, and it was time for both of them to get to work.

Problem was, how could she work when Hannah's assignment was rolling around in her brain? Learn what truth is.

She sat at her desk, pulled out a notepad, and wrote "Truth" at the top.

"Excuse me."

Startled, Ronnie looked up. Hannah's first real patient for the day had somehow snuck in without a peep. Maybe that was part of the problem he was dealing with.

"I'll let Hannah know you're here." She pressed a speaker button to let Hannah know her first patient had arrived. Hannah. Not Dr. Ernst, a title she'd earned—that was truth—but she preferred being called "Hannah" because most patients felt more comfortable around her without the title. Was that truth? It wasn't a fact, just an observation. To discern what was the truth, they'd have to do a study and that wasn't happening.

Seconds later, Hannah's door opened. She welcomed in the patient, then closed the door for privacy. More truth. A closed door in this office meant privacy for doctor and patient. That was easy.

Ronnie looked down at her pad and double underlined the word "Truth." Then she wrote names below it.

Dad

Mom

Gavin

Kyle

She hesitated before writing one more, but really, this might be the biggest of all. She wrote down two words:

The church

Honestly, that was the deal breaker. If what she'd learned at church wasn't true, then was there really any truth at all?

Chapter Five

Sunday...

Ronnie sat up in bed, blankets wrapped around her, though June's heat penetrated the apartment walls. She hadn't missed a church service in years. If not at True North, then somewhere else. Camp, college chapel, Grandma Eva's church.

And what had she learned all those years?

Not a whole lot. Of course, she hadn't been an active listener either. When your dad is preaching, you tend to turn off the words. Other PKs she knew all said the same thing. Many of those same PKs had become prodigals. Others became preachers.

And her? She didn't know what she'd become. Just a robot going to church on Sunday because that was expected of her.

Maybe she should stay in bed today, thumb her finger at God for making a mess of her life. Okay, so He hadn't created the mess, but He certainly hadn't stopped it. Hadn't gotten out His vacuum and dust rag to clean everything but left it to her.

Dad was home. Alone.

Mom had moved, but Grandma Eva wasn't happy.

Gavin called her every day. She avoided him every day. Yet, he always left a simple message: Veronica, I love you.

Words from a plain-speaking neurologist. Were they the truth?

Maybe, but truth was more than words. That was one thing she'd discerned this week. If someone says, "I love you," but spends all their spare time on the computer, the truth was that they loved the computer more.

And what about God's role in all this? She looked toward her ceiling. "Do You hear me?"

Silence answered, but then she'd ignored Him all week, not that that was any different from before her dad was arrested. When it came to faith, Kyle had been the same as her. They'd been a PK and a worship minister living together but not married. Apart from church they hadn't prayed together. What that told her was that neither she nor Kyle were real Christ followers.

At least they hadn't been. Kyle had changed since their breakup, from a man who basically wore a worship minister costume to work, to a man who lived out that work in his everyday life.

Did he believe?

What did she believe?

She looked upward again, searched the ceiling as if she'd see God there. "I don't know You. I never have." She felt that admission in her churning gut. "If You are real, can

You show me?"

Maybe instead of asking a wimpy question, she should make a demand. But that didn't feel right.

What did feel right, though, was getting up and going to church. Not True North. Even that church's name was a lie. She doubted she'd ever return.

Now, what was the name of Kyle's church? She removed her phone from the bedside charger and scrolled through her contacts.

New Hope. Down in Northfield. A good hour away. Would she have time to make it to a service? There were plenty of churches near her, but if this one had changed Kyle, maybe she'd learn truth from them as well.

Ronnie snuck into the back pew of the church. How old fashioned was this place that it still had pews? True North had gotten rid of theirs by the time she was old enough to be welcomed into the adult service, and that was more than a couple decades ago.

Kyle was up on the stage—well, it really wasn't a stage here—but whatever they called the place the pastor spoke from. Anyway, Kyle was there playing keyboard and singing a tune she knew from True North. No band, just his new girlfriend playing guitar in the background.

To think he gave up True North for this rinky-dink gig. At True North, he'd had a full band behind him, along with flashing lights, and massive speakers that shook the building. Attending church had been like going to a rock concert, drawing hundreds of young people. Here, with all the people—mostly grey-hairs—singing, she could barely hear Kyle.

She felt like she was at *church*. Without thinking, she wrinkled her nose.

Wait. Wasn't that the point? How much had she learned about God at True North with all its flashiness?

Convicted already, and all she'd done was criticize Kyle's so-called band.

So what if she could barely hear him sing? Wasn't that the point?

She closed her eyes and listened, found herself singing along to a song about the great "I Am." In the past, she hadn't paid attention to the lyrics. She'd sung, hands raised, because that was what you did at a concert.

But church wasn't a concert.

She concentrated on the words, listened to those singing around her, caught snippets of Kyle's voice above the others. Of the girlfriend singing harmony. He'd never known how jealous she'd been of that old girlfriend when they'd all gone to True North. The ten years Ronnie had lived with Kyle, not once had his eyes lit up like they did around Trip.

Maybe the truth was, Kyle had never loved Ronnie, that he'd always loved Trip. Now that those two were back together, maybe that was why he was a changed man.

The Kyle she'd lived with had loved the attention of being

on stage, but this Kyle seemed content to blend into the background.

Another change for him.

The song ended and she waited for one of Kyle's over-the-top prayers, but it didn't come. Instead, a different voice spoke a prayer over the room. She snuck a glance at the preacher, expecting to see him in a robe. He wasn't. But he also wasn't dressed like a hipster as some of the associate pastors at True North dressed.

The pastor started speaking, talking about a loving God. Ha! So loving, that her entire family was a mess.

She'd heard enough, seen enough for the day. Maybe her truth was that she didn't need or want God. Others could believe what they wanted. She got up and slipped out the back door. Leaving early, she'd also probably avoid Kyle.

But if she stayed, she'd get to see Evie.

Seeing her ex would be worth it.

"Ronnie?"

Her breath hitched at the sound of his voice. Okay, maybe seeing him wasn't worth it. She turned toward his voice and her gaze immediately flew to Kyle's arm stretched behind Trip's back.

"What are you doing here?" That wasn't the friendly greeting she expected from this changed man.

She raised her chin. "Can't a woman see her daughter?"

He whispered something in Trip's ear. She smiled at him and walked away, probably eager to escape the tension zipping through the lobby.

Several feet remained between her and Kyle. Should she

make the first move to bridge the gap? Nah. She crossed her arms. Let him do it.

A couple of silent seconds ticked away before he took a couple steps toward her, his gaze examining her face as if expecting her to pull some kind of stunt. That was her dad's *modus operandi*, not hers.

He splayed his hands. Offering an olive branch? "She'd love to see you. I was just going to pick her up from the nursery. Follow me."

Her breath hitched. Until this moment, she hadn't realized how very much she missed her daughter. She followed Kyle, but all she could think about was holding Evie, smelling the berries in her hair, feeling those pudgy arms around her neck.

He opened a door and gestured for her to enter.

"Momma, Momma, Momma."

Her hand flew to her chest. "Baby girl, how are you?" Ronnie began unlocking the hinged door separating the children from the sign-in desk.

A wrinkled, female hand held it closed.

Ronnie would tell her a thing or two. She looked up at an elderly woman, who appeared ready to take on God's entire army.

"You don't have signed permission to pick her up."

"As you can see, Evie's father is right—"

"Ronnie." He rested a hand on her shoulder. "Let me check her out. When it comes to our children, Donna is strict about following protocol. You and I are both grateful for that."

How dare he speak for her?

She opened her mouth to spew more awful words, but common sense finally took over and she locked her mouth closed before she could stick her foot in any further.

"I'm sorry." She smiled at the woman, as Kyle signed the form. Donna had transformed somehow from an army general to a doting grandmother. "It's just been too long since I've seen her, and I'm over eager."

"Oh, I understand." Donna unlocked the door and Evie pushed through right into Ronnie's legs.

She grabbed hold as if she'd fall from a cliff if she let go.

Ronnie knelt and scooped up her daughter, who squeezed her arms around Ronnie's neck. She breathed in the...what? Minty, not strawberry scent of her hair. So, Kyle was changing things up. Guess that was his prerogative.

She carried Evie from the nursery to the still empty lobby, not ever wanting to let go of her daughter again. Tonight was officially the end of Kyle's time. Maybe he'd be okay with her taking Evie home—

"Before you get it in that head of yours, Evie stays with me until tonight. Trip and I have plans with her."

Trip and Kyle had plans with her daughter? "Do you think that's smart, her getting used to Trip being around? What happens when you two break up? That'll just be one more person ripped from Evie's life."

He laughed at her! "You gave up the right to have a say in my life when you walked out the door on us."

"That was before I had Evie."

He just raised his brows. Okay, the truth was—there was

that word again—the truth was she was pregnant with Evie when she'd walked out, enticed by greener grass. Turned out Gavin was merely AstroTurf, not the real thing.

"Okay, fine, so I was already pregnant, but shouldn't we discuss important changes in our lives that affect our daughter?" She was parroting that from someone, but she couldn't remember who.

He laughed again. "Huh, I said that when you started dating Mr. Brain Doc, but you claimed it was your life, and I had no say."

"You said that?" Oh boy. Suddenly Evie grew heavy in her arms, so she looked for a place to sit.

"What's going on, Ronnie?" His voice trailed behind her as she numbly followed her feet to the fellowship hall set up with rows of tables and chairs.

She pulled out a chair and sat, keeping Evie tucked tightly in her arms. Kyle pulled out the chair across from her, spun it halfway around, then straddled the back.

"I down." Evie struggled to be let go, but Ronnie couldn't force her arms to release.

"I'm sure it's been a tough week."

It was Ronnie's turn to laugh. "Oh, it was a piece of cake. Dad's all over the news. True North is imploding. Mom moved in with Grandma Eva, who doesn't want Mom there. She better not try to move in with me. Gavin and I are...I don't know what we are. And now I show up at your church and you're all cozy with your former girlfriend."

He just smirked. "Are you done?"

Done with people, that was for certain. "All I want is

some extra time with Evie before I go to work tomorrow. Is that too much to ask?"

His features softened. "I'm sorry. I'm being a jerk."

Did he just apologize? Foreign words from the Kyle she knew.

He really had changed.

"And I'm not being much better." There, she could apologize too. Sort of.

"Truce?"

She nodded then shook her head. "This shouldn't be so hard. I'd give anything to have an intact family and not shuffle Evie around." Out of the corner of her eye, she glimpsed Trip speaking with the pastor, and the ugly green monster reared up inside. "Are you and Trip serious?"

A silly grin that reminded her of a high-school boy crush, blossomed on his face. Ronnie had never seen that look for her.

"Yeah. We are. Of course, we're just getting reacquainted. We'll see how the summer goes."

So that meant she had time yet. "What if..." She extended her hand across the table, but he didn't take the bait. "What if we tried to work things out? Give Evie that family she deserves?"

His face contorted in a way she couldn't read. "Ronnie, you're married."

"But, only for a couple of days—"

"No." He got up and slid the chair beneath the table. "You closed that door on our family when you walked out on me. You locked it for good last weekend when you and

Brain Doc—"

"Gavin."

"Whatever. When you got married. This conversation is over." He held open his arms to her daughter, who too eagerly went to him. "You can pick her up tonight at six."

The two strode away, leaving her sitting alone in a strange church, a place she clearly didn't belong. She grabbed her purse and aimed for the doors leading outside.

"You must be Veronica."

She stopped at the sound of the pastor's distinctive voice. She could be rude and just walk away—after all, he didn't know her—but parental training forced her to stop and be polite. She spun around and put on the plaster smile she'd perfected at True North.

"And you're the pastor."

"Mitch." He extended his hand. "Nice to meet you."

Right. "You know, pastor, I understand lying is against one of the Ten Commandments." She may not remember much of her Sunday school learning, but everyone knew about Moses and the commandments.

He laughed, right from the belly, and kept his hand extended. "As I said, it's nice to meet you. And I really mean that."

"Really?" Color her skeptical, but no doubt Kyle had spilled out every rotten thing she'd ever done to him, which was plenty.

"Kyle speaks highly of you. Says you're a great mom to Evelyn."

She almost laughed at that. "I'm not certain we're

speaking about the same person."

He laughed again. "Have a moment? I'd love to talk with you."

Sure, she had a moment. All day, in fact, but she glanced at her watch anyway to make a show of being short for time.

Definitely not truthful. If she wanted to explore truth, it should probably start with her.

"Actually, I have all afternoon open. I was hoping to get Evie now, but that didn't work out." She glimpsed her daughter now holding Trip's hand and had to tamp down her jealousy.

"I'm sorry for that." He gestured toward the table she'd just escaped from. "Can I get you a refreshment? Coffee? Water? Donut?"

She looked around for a coffee bar with made-to-order drinks like True North had, and her gaze landed on a table on the far side of the room. Coffee was poured from metal dispensers and not created by a barista. The table was filled with a variety of donuts, none that would be kind to her figure, and no fruit choices. This place would never attract the young seeker.

As she didn't wish to offend the pastor, she would make do with what was available. "I'll take a coffee with cream, please."

"Coming right up."

He scooted toward the serving table, getting stopped several times along the way by parishioners wishing to speak with him. Each time, the conversation was quick and amiable. How did he do that without angering the people he was putting off?

Shortly after, he arrived back at her table with two cups of coffee and two chocolate covered donuts.

"Brought you a donut just in case you change your mind. Our local bakery whips them up for us on Sunday morning, so they're fresh."

"And if I don't change my mind?" Which she wouldn't.

He shrugged and grinned. "Guess I get two donuts, although my wife might have a thing or ten to say about that." He took a long sip of his coffee and sighed. "Just want I needed."

Then he folded his hands on the table and made eye contact with her. "First, I want to say how sorry I am for your family's troubles. Not an easy thing to go through."

Kyle had gossiped about her family?

He held up both hands as if he'd read her mind. "Kyle has said nothing other than that his daughter's mother is the daughter of True North's senior pastor. With the news, I put two and two together."

And got four. Truth.

"Know that I and the local pastors I meet with are all praying for your family. We feel a special kinship with those who get in trouble publicly, knowing each of us is susceptible to sin that could land us in the same position."

How did she respond to that? All she could muster was a quiet, "Thank you."

"I'm curious then, what brings you to our church? Your daughter?"

She could say, "Yes, to see Evie," but that would be a lie.

"Honestly, it was the change in Kyle. I wanted to see for myself what prompted that change." She glanced around the fellowship hall and across the way at the old-fashioned sanctuary, none of which matched the attention-starved man she once knew. Two plus two was equaling five.

"Aw, you're wondering how a church that appears to be a few decades behind can affect a change in a young person."

It was if he'd read her mind, but the words certainly weren't flattering coming from his lips. Made her sound arrogant.

She probably was, but she'd use that as a stepping point. "How do you attract my generation?"

"That requires visual stimulation?" He scanned the room, then grinned. "We're a work in progress, but to be honest we don't try too hard to look like the world. The most important thing is that we worship God. That we believe Jesus is the 'Great I Am,' as the song spoke of this morning. It wasn't New Hope that changed Kyle. It was all Jesus."

"I still don't understand. He was a worship leader at one of the Twin Cities' largest churches, but he wasn't the man he is now."

"Just because you work in a church, pray in front of people, sing words of praise, doesn't mean you follow Christ."

Each of his words was a dart directed right at her heart.

And at her father. "Do you doubt my father's beliefs?"

He looked up and stared at some random spot on the

ceiling as if having a silent conversation with it before focusing back on her.

"I didn't know your father. I can't speak for his heart, his beliefs—that's up to God and God alone. But I do know that, as Christians, we all sin, we all have moments of failure, times when our actions and words hurt God's kingdom. That doesn't mean we don't believe. It just means we're human and a work in progress. And we're forgiven."

"So there's hope for my father?"

"Yes, there's always hope, and Jesus is our living hope."

It was her turn to look away, stare at a blot on the wall. There was hope for her father, and that was good. But what about her? True North frequently had messages of love and hope, but all this talk about Jesus had her shimmying in her chair.

"Um, this might be a silly question from a PK, but what about those who have other truths? Those who follow God, but not Jesus. That's not me, I mean, I believe in Jesus, but isn't it narrowminded to say everyone should believe what I do?"

There, she'd stated what really burdened her heart.

"Hmm." He took out his phone and started scrolling through it. "That's a question so many have today, and I appreciate you having the courage to ask it." He set down his phone and looked across the table. "Can I give you an assignment?"

Another assignment? What was with people?

"You can give me one, but I won't promise I'll do it."

"Fair enough. I promise, I won't grade you."

You probably won't ever see me again, either.

"Sure. Fine. Give me your assignment."

He held up a finger. "Wait here, please." He rushed off to somewhere in the church and came back minutes later with a tablet and a pen. He started writing something down.

"We live in a mixed-up world, with tons of information being tossed at us with all the media outlets, and sometimes it's difficult to glean the truth out of all that information." He tore the piece of paper from the tablet and handed it to her.

"You were wondering about Kyle, what caused his change. For him, it was digging into the Bible, understanding it from a different perspective. He stopped seeing the Bible as a book of rules and stories, but rather a living, breathing document. A love letter from God, if you will."

She stared down at the piece of paper in her hand. "Look up 'I Am' statements in the Bible." No surprise, coming from a minister.

"You want truth? You want to know who Jesus is compared to the other small G gods out there?" He tapped the paper with his finger. "These are seven 'I Am' statements from the Bible. If you want to know the truth about who Jesus is, the truth about other gods, this is a good place to start." He looked up at the ceiling again and nodded as if in a conversation with someone.

"And one more thing." He took back the piece of paper and wrote something else on it. "Before reading the 'I Am' statements, read John one, one through five to understand what the Bible really is."

What the Bible is? "I'm sorry, you've lost me now."

"That's okay. Do your homework. I have a feeling you'll find your way back."

Somehow it seemed as if they were talking about two different things.

He checked his watch. "Thanks for talking with me. My phone number's on the sheet there if you have any questions. But for now, my lovely bride is expecting me home. I've learned if I want a hot meal, I need to arrive on time."

He walked away before she crumpled the note. She hadn't come here for a Bible school class, but had needed to see the place that had changed Kyle.

None of it added up.

She stood and walked toward the front door of the church, checking to see if Evie was still around anywhere. A goodbye hug would certainly have been nice, even if they were going to see each other tonight, but there was no sign of the too-cozy family. She walked past a garbage can and threw out the pastor's assignment.

She was a pastor's daughter, for Pete's sake. She didn't need someone else to preach to her about the Bible and what was truth. She'd grown up with it.

But then why did everything in her life go so wrong?

Chapter Six

Ronnie shut her car door and stared at the front door of Kyle's home. She hated this part of being a broken family. Shuffling their daughter between homes so Evie would have no real home. She'd always be caught in the middle of whatever drama her parents were going through. They'd be lucky if she didn't grow up completely messed up.

And whose fault is that?

She shoved the thought aside and hurried to the front door. She jabbed the doorbell harder than she intended to, but taking her frustrations out on the doorbell rather than on Kyle wouldn't be a bad thing.

The door flung open and Kyle waved her inside, gestured to the mini suitcase by the door. "She's all ready."

"Momma, Momma, Momma." Evie toddled toward her, her arms upstretched.

Ronnie lifted her daughter, and just like that her anger and disappointments melted away. Yesterday couldn't be changed, but Evie's future would be determined by how Ronnie and Kyle behaved today, and she was intent on making a positive impact.

"How was she?" Ronnie kissed her baby girl's nearly-bald head.

"The best." Kyle rubbed Evie's back. "We saw tigers today."

"Tigers?" Speaking in a childlike voice, Ronnie held Evie out so she could see her expression. "Did you see tigers?"

Evie nodded vigorously.

"And what does the tiger say, Cadenza?" Kyle asked, using his pet name for Evie.

Evie's face crumpled up, her attempt at looking mean, but it made her even cuter. "Woarrr."

"That must have been a powerful tiger," Ronnie said.

Her eyes wide, Evie nodded.

"Time to go home?"

"Dada Gabin?"

Hearing that nearly broke her heart. "No, baby girl, we won't see Dada Gavin tonight." Though he still called daily. "Just you and me."

Evie's tiny little lip perched outward. "Dada Gabin."

She sighed and hugged Evie close. Would it hurt to have him visit?

Sure, and add one more adult into her daughter's already fragmented life. It was best to make a clean break so they could all move forward.

"Say bye-bye to Dada."

"Wuv Dada." She reached out her arms and gave his neck a squeeze.

"Love you too, Cadenza." He kissed her cheek and looked

at the floor, but not before she saw a glisten in his eyes.

Time to head home before everyone's heart broke.

She picked up Evie's suitcase and turned to the door.

"I saw you talking with Pastor Mitch this morning."

Huh? She spun toward him. "What's that to you?"

He shrugged. "Just an observation. He's a good man. I learned a lot from him. Gives me assignments all the time."

"He gave me an assignment as well." That she wished she hadn't thrown away. Why was she so emotionally impulsive?

"I recommend following through. He's got good insights."

"I'll think about it." She turned away again. "See you in two weeks?"

"Yeah." His voice softened. "Two weeks. See you at your place."

"Actually, pick her up at my old apartment." She was glad she couldn't see Kyle's face and the judgment she'd see there.

Silence, then, "Sure. See you in two weeks."

Ronnie walked out the door, Evie cuddled tight against her as if she'd never let go. Two weeks here. Two weeks there. And back again. No stability. Unlike the home Ronnie had grown up in.

Mom claimed the marriage had been over years ago, but Ronnie hadn't seen that. She'd witnessed two people love each other and her. Was she blind that she hadn't seen her father's faults?

After buckling Evie into her car seat, she looked up at the

cloud-dappled sky and whispered a prayer. "If You're up there, if You really exist, can You open my eyes to see the truth?"

Home.

Why was that word so depressing?

Evie held onto Ronnie's fingers as they walked into the apartment. It was a luxury place, with an elevator and all the updated amenities besides the pool and fitness center. The complex had a coffee bar, a car wash, a media room, and so much more. Everything she needed.

So why didn't it feel like home?

She opened the door to her apartment and Evie ran in, right to her stash of toys. She was more at home here than Ronnie was.

But at least Evie was here, and her bubbly enthusiasm filled the place that had been too quiet last week. Maybe that was why Ronnie was so ruminative today—she'd spent too much time speaking to herself.

She carried Evie's suitcase to the nursery, and her phone pinged, showing she had a message from the apartment concierge. Someone had dropped off flowers.

Flowers? Who would do that?

Still, she messaged back as she walked into her living room, and said to bring them up. Maybe someone from True North sent them, hoping to brighten her day. Really, it was odd that so few people from church had contacted her. Along with her father, she'd become a pariah to that community. Weren't churches supposed to be there for you when life went south?

How often were you there for others at True North?

The thought smacked her in the conscience, and she fell hard on her living room couch. She'd been too busy, too important to serve others, and trusted designated small groups to handle church attendees' struggles. She'd even scorned her mother for helping, telling her she was taking away someone else's job.

Right. Like the person or group whose job it was to reach out to her. Guess consigning others to do a small job was always the easiest thing to do. But not the right thing. Maybe those "small" people-connecting tasks weren't so small after all. Once she established herself in a new church, serving their membership was the first thing she'd sign up for.

With her dad's incarceration, her eyes were being opened.

Huh. Was that her prayer back at Kyle's, about God opening her eyes to the truth, being answered?

The doorbell rang, and she leaped off the couch, eager to see who had remembered her. Evie scooted past her and tried opening the door.

"Uh-uh, baby girl. Momma gets the door." Holding Evie back with one hand, she opened the door with the other.

The concierge stood there with a single purple hyacinth in a vase. It was gorgeous.

"Who is it from?" she mused out loud but didn't get an answer as the concierge hurried to another task.

"Fwower?" Evie tried reaching for it.

"A pretty flower." A very specific flower, she was certain. Not something generic most people would send. This one was intentionally chosen. Of that she was certain.

She shut the door and carried it to the dining table. She set it down and shifted it around to get just the right angle before removing the full-sized card from the vase.

"Come here, sweetie, let's see who it's from."

Evie followed her to the couch and climbed up on her lap. She reached for the card as Ronnie pulled it from the envelope, and a letter fell out.

A letter with Gavin's handwriting.

The card had watercolor flowers cascading down the side, with the simple words, "Sorry I hurt you" on the front. Inside was blank but for his signature. Simple, but to the point. Very Gavin like.

"I see." Evie grabbed the card, scrunching it in her chubby hands.

"It's from Dada Gavin."

"I see Dada Gabin."

A four-word sentence? Oh my! She had to tell...Who? Gavin? Mom? Dad? Certainly not Kyle. He'd rightly put her in her place this morning when she'd absurdly brought up them getting back together. Of course, that couldn't happen—time and distance had shown her how ridiculous that notion had been.

But reconciling with Gavin...was that just as silly?

Evie slid from her lap, the card from Gavin clutched in her hand. A child's way of demonstrating her love? Ronnie had no clue. About anything.

She made herself comfortable on the couch, sitting so she could keep an eye on Evie, and unfolded the tri-fold letter.

Veronica,

She did love how he used her full name as a term of endearment.

Did I ever tell you about the couple I recently met who've been married 70 years?

Gavin may not be loquacious, but he loved telling stories about people he met through work. To him, those were love notes. And she missed them.

Yes, seven-zero. I think they married in their late teens. Can you imagine that kind of commitment?

Honestly, no, she couldn't. Not anymore. Not if her parents made it to forty years and split. There was hope for them yet, right?

Anyway, "Billy" has a form of dementia, so "Delores" has been his caregiver since his diagnosis. I learn so much just by listening to them. He doesn't always know her, but she always loves him. Sometimes he thinks she's his nurse from back when he served in the Korean War. She doesn't try to correct him, just goes with the flow. Sometimes he tells others in the care center that he has a new girlfriend. Instead of correcting him, she flirts. And then there are the few times when he's cognizant of who she is, and those moments nearly have her weeping. But through it all, she loves him.

Ronnie sniffled and reached for a tissue on the side table.

Why this story? It made me think of us.

Us? In what way did this beautiful couple resemble her and Gavin?

Ah, I can see your wrinkled forehead as you try to figure this out.

And that made her smile.

Actually, it made me consider my own faulty actions.

Okay, now we're getting somewhere.

First, let me say "I'm sorry." Obviously, I let you down when I thought I was protecting you. I thought concealing the truth was safer than being honest.

When you confronted me last Tuesday, the truth was revealed to me. Yes, your father encouraged me to marry you last weekend, said it would enable you to get full custody of Evie. It was the shove I needed to make it happen.

As for the offering of a spot on the board. Yes, it's true he added in that enticement, but it was immediately rebuffed. If I'm to get on the board, which is my wish, I will do it through the proper channels.

And the reasoning behind my desire for being on the board is what I hid from you. You see, as I've been studying the Bible, elements of worship and church leadership at True North bothered me. I sensed a drifting from the Word into a nebulous place that welcomed all and judged none. Sounds utopian to the outsider—it did to me when I first joined as a new believer. But I've learned that Utopia doesn't intersect with God's Kingdom. I desired to see more truth-telling and less, for lack of a better term, wishy-washyness. From my perspective, it appeared that True North had strayed from both being truthful and pointing northward.

That made her want to laugh and cry at the same time. She'd love to hear the phrase *wishy-washy* come from his lips. She didn't have a clue that he'd been unhappy with True North's teaching. She never had a problem with it.

Perhaps it reminded me of the church in Laodicea that was described as lukewarm. I felt that to sit by and do nothing was wrong and the best way to share my input was through the board. Though your father's offer was an enticement, it played no part in my proposal to you. In fact, I rejected it with perhaps too much irritation.

So, that is the reason I did not inform you of your father's offer. I did not wish to hurt you by sharing my feelings about True North, a place I know you loved. A place that was home to you. How could I squelch that love in you? Now I realize that in not revealing the truth, I was being as "wishy-washy" as True North.

I hope you can forgive me.

With all my love,

Gavin

She laid the letter down on her lap. Evie, with a toy stethoscope draped around her neck, still clutched the card from Gavin.

Could she forgive him?

Oh, yes. But there was more to his note than desiring

forgiveness. He was pointing fingers at her church home. Yes, it had problems, but he was expressing concern over theological matters, which meant he was pointing fingers at her father.

In essence, Gavin called both True North and her father liars.

Even with her father's arrest, she didn't know how to reconcile that.

"Baby girl." She waved to Evie. "Come here. Momma needs a hug."

Evie hurried over and climbed onto Ronnie's lap. How she had been blessed with a child so even tempered, so placid, Ronnie didn't know, but she was grateful, especially now. Evie's temperament was the only piece of Ronnie's life that wasn't throwing fits.

She took out her phone. Hovered over Gavin's name. Should she? Was she ready to speak with him, hear his perspective?

Her thumb reflexively pressed down, and the phone dialed out. It wasn't too late to hang up, but then he'd probably call right back. Maybe she should pull up her big girl pants and speak with him.

It rang and rang and rang five times before his voice mail picked up and she blew out a held breath as she ended the call. Chances were, he was working or volunteering. He did a lot of both.

Would he call back?

Not something she planned to worry about. When or if he called, she'd deal with it then. Hopefully, she'd have her feelings worked out.

The phone rang just as Ronnie laid her head on her pillow. Gavin? Nerves and excitement fought for the lead as she reached for her phone on the bedstand.

But the caller I.D. didn't say *Gavin*. It read *Dad*.

She fumbled the phone and it fell to the floor, continuing to ring. Did she want to talk with him? *Yes*. And *no*. She wanted to talk with Dad, the man who adored her, the man who could do no wrong.

But he was broken, fallible, and she didn't know what to say to that man. She didn't trust him? True. She was angry? Definitely.

Her heart broke for him? Unquestionably.

God, what do I do?

Funny how until this incident, she hadn't been in the habit of praying. Now today, she'd sent up two prayers without stepping a foot over True North's threshold.

She reached down for the phone, and it stopped ringing. No matter, she'd call him right back, but the phone pinged, indicating he'd left a voice mail. She hit the app and brought up his message.

"Veronica, dear, I know this week's been tough on you. It's been rough on us all. I'm a better man than the world's seen. Looks like I'll get off with a fine. I can deal with that. Before you know it, I'll be back in the pulpit preaching to thousands. I guarantee it. Hoping to see you soon. Love you to the stars and back."

Ronnie set the phone down on her bed. Something disturbed her about the message, but she couldn't determine what.

What she did know was that she didn't plan to return her father's call tonight. Maybe tomorrow when she was fully awake.

But something told her that being awake would make his message seem far worse than it did tonight.

Chapter Seven

om...mom." Cough, cough. "Mom...mom."

Hurtful sobs awoke Ronnie. She glanced at her phone. Five in the morning? A full two hours before Ronnie would normally wake Evie up. No doubt, she was feeling the tension from this upheaval as well.

Ronnie dragged herself from the bed and shuffled to Evie's room, to the crib.

"Hey, baby girl, Momma's here."

Evie continued to cry and cough, so Ronnie laid the back of her hand on her child's forehead. Oh, my, she was burning up. No wonder she was crying.

She hurried with Evie to the bathroom and scanned her child's forehead. One hundred point two. Not enough to warrant going to the doctor, but definitely hot enough to avoid daycare. Wonderful. Mondays were crazy-busy, and though Hannah was always understanding, Ronnie still hated inconveniencing her. One of the drawbacks of being a two-person business. But Evie always came first. If Kyle lived closer, she'd give him a call, but he now lived an hour away. And Mom was an hour in the other direction, staying with Grandma Eva. Leaving Evie with Dad wasn't an option.

"Baby girl." She kissed Evie's water-stained cheek. "Momma's going to make a phone call. I need to set you down for a moment."

Evie clung on even tighter and buried her head in the crook of Ronnie's neck. Guess she'd just have to talk over the sobs.

She called Hannah, who naturally said it wasn't a problem, when Ronnie knew it was. Still she was grateful for an employer who was willing to work with the challenges of single motherhood. Then she called her daycare provider, who would get paid for the day, even though she didn't have to watch Evie. Finally, Ronnie carried Evie, coughing and sobbing, into the master bedroom to lie down together. She didn't want Evie to get in the habit of sleeping in her bed, but when she was sick, Ronnie made the exception.

Moments later, thumb in mouth, Evie was asleep at Ronnie's side. There was nothing like baby cuddles to make a woman feel important. Loved.

Well, maybe except for lying next to your husband.

"Gavin, I miss you," she whispered to the darkness.

Did she? Did she really miss Gavin? Or was it the letters attached to his name? The massive home he'd inherited from his parents? His sizable bank account?

Unease soured in her stomach.

His looks hadn't attracted her at the beginning. To be

honest, they'd turned her off. Sure he was tall, but those glasses and that haircut and his wardrobe screamed geek, and she'd been too cool to date someone like that. Besides, she was living with Kyle back then, so she hadn't been looking.

But when Dad added "Neurologist" to the introduction, well, that had changed her perspective.

Made her sick to her stomach to think how shallow she'd been.

She looked around her bedroom, furnished with the finest, thanks to Gavin. Her wardrobe wasn't lacking, thanks to Gavin.

Did she love him or his bank account? Did she love how impressed her equally-shallow friends had been when she spoke about her then fiancé?

She kissed Evie's cheek and cuddled her closer. This was love. Real, selfless love. Ronnie would do anything for this child. But would she do anything for Gavin? Had she avoided marriage because she'd secretly been looking for a way out of the relationship? Was this the truth that Hannah had alluded to concerning Gavin?

The answer made her want to throw up.

Which meant later today, she'd give him a call, invite him over, apologize, and set him free.

It was the right thing to do. Maybe the first right choice she'd made as an adult. Made her want to add her own tears to Evie's.

Bzzz. Bzzz. Bzzz.

What? Ronnie blinked herself awake to the sound of her phone buzzing, the sound made when someone wanted to be let in.

She checked the time. Nine o'clock? She never slept this long. Beside her, Evie still slept. Ronnie kissed her forehead. It had cooled considerably.

Bzzz. Bzzz. Bzzz.

Oh, and someone was at her door. She answered her cell, "This is Ronnie."

"And this is your mother. Hannah said you didn't come in today."

So you just stop by for a visit? Nice. She rolled her eyes.

"I'll buzz you in." She pressed in the code to open the door for Mom, then looked down at her nightshirt. Oh, Mom was going to have a field day with her still being in her pajamas. Well, tough. Mom wasn't dealing with a sick child.

She got up, ran her fingers through her hair, and went to the kitchen to prep the coffee maker. She checked the fridge for anything to feed Mom, but it was nearly as empty as Old Mother Hubbard's cupboard. Grocery shopping was on today's to-do list.

A knock sounded on the door, and Ronnie hurried to open it.

Mom was there, naturally, but so was a large suitcase and a couple small ones. "Surprise! Guess who's coming to live with you!"

Ronnie choked and struggled to get out, "Say what?"

"Excuse me." Mom took the handle of the big suitcase. "Can you grab those for me, please?"

"Uh...sure." Speechless, she followed Mom through the living room into the third bedroom, which Ronnie had used as her office.

"Have you washed the sheets lately?" Mom lifted the comforter.

"Not lately, but after a friend stayed the night a few months ago."

"No problem. I'll wash them."

"Now just wait a second." Ronnie finally found her voice. "I didn't invite you here, and I certainly didn't say you could stay."

"You expect me to stay with your father?"

Actually, yes. "What about Grandma Eva?"

Mom huffed. "She told me to go home. Work on my marriage. She has no idea what life has been like living with the pompous windbag."

Whoa. Ronnie stepped back, startled. She'd never heard her mom call anyone names, much less her father. She'd never seen her mother so aggressive, so assertive. On other women that was a good look, but on Mom? She was supposed to smile and have patience and always be kind.

What ridiculous expectations. It was a wonder Mom hadn't cracked earlier.

Still, Ronnie did not want this living arrangement to last too long.

"Okay. You're welcome to stay until other plans can be made."

"That's generous of you." Definitely said with a sarcastic lilt.

Ronnie couldn't rein herself in. "You're not the only one dealing with the fall-out of Dad's actions. In case you haven't noticed, your marriage isn't the only one on the line."

Mom sighed and sat hard on the bed. "I know," she said, barely above a whisper. "And I'm sorry you're going through this."

"Me too." Ronnie sat beside her mother and cuddled against her side like Evie had earlier this morning. "We're quite the pair."

"Tell me about it." Mom perked up and looked out the door. "Where's my granddaughter? Hannah said she was ill?"

"She woke up this morning with a cough and a low-grade fever. She's doing better already. It's like someone knew you'd be stopping in today, so I needed to be home."

"Someone…" Mom stared off at nothing. "A couple weeks ago, I would have cheerfully told you that's a God incident. What a bunch of malarky."

Had Mom thrown away her faith? She couldn't. Ronnie needed her mom to be strong. "I'm sorry Dad hurt you like this."

"What have you got for breakfast?" Mom stood without acknowledging Ronnie.

Okay. She could take the hint. No mentioning Dad. For

now, anyway. "Not much. Today's my shopping day."

"You don't have it delivered?" Mom aimed for the kitchen.

"The shoppers aren't as choosy about fruits and vegetables as I am."

"You always were picky."

Appreciate the compliment...

"Gama?" Evie entered the living room, dragging a blanket behind her.

"Oh, there's my precious Evelyn."

Leave it to Evie to add a smile to Mom's face. Breakfast for the adults was quickly forgotten as Mom lifted Evie and gave her a lingering hug.

"You're just the medicine I need." Mom kissed Evie, who coughed. "Oh, dear, do you have a cold?"

"I cough." Evie forced a fake cough, the little stinker. "I sweep Momma."

"You sleep with your momma? Not all the time I hope."

Oh, Mom moving in was going to be a load of fun.

"No. Not all the time. Just last night when she was running a fever and coughing."

Mom kissed Evie's forehead. "Hmm. Doesn't seem to have a fever now. Maybe you were mistaken."

"And maybe I know exactly what I'm doing." She couldn't ever remember talking back, but Ronnie refused to be put down, especially in front of her own daughter. "I'm a good mother."

Mom plopped down on the couch, keeping Evie on her lap. "Yes, you are. I'm sorry. I seem to have lost my filter." She sighed. "Forgive me?"

"I think we're both going to have to make use of stronger filters as long as you're here."

"That's probably true. Now." She set Evie down, slapped her legs, and stood. "Time for you to head in to work while Evie and I enjoy our day together."

Ronnie was about to ask, "Are you sure?" but then common sense prevailed. Naturally, Mom wanted a day with her favorite and only granddaughter.

Wait…"So does this mean I have a built-in babysitter as long as you're here?"

"I have to earn my keep somehow."

"It's a deal."

Maybe having her mother around all the time wouldn't be such a bad thing after all.

Ronnie awoke to the sound of pots clanging in the kitchen. She could not wait until her mother found a new place to live, and she'd only been here a week. Six days of hearing how rotten her father was. Six days of being told how to mother. Six days of fighting for attention from Evie.

This had to stop. Soon. Or Ronnie would go bonkers.

She sat up in bed, resigning herself to no more sleep.

How could she convince her mother to leave? Through getting her parents back together again? Considering how Mom pretty much hated Dad's guts right now, that wasn't going to be easy, but if Ronnie ever wanted her home back, she was willing to try anything.

A knock on her door. Then it opened. Didn't even give Ronnie time to yell, "Stay out."

Mom walked in with a vase of pink and red carnations. "Delivery for you."

"Who would send me flowers?"

Mom's brows popped up.

Yeah. Gavin. Duh.

Mom set the vase on the window table then handed the envelope to Ronnie.

She opened the envelope and found another no-frills card with the words, "I miss you" inscribed on the front. Inside, another folded letter and his messy signature. Simple and to the point, just like the man.

How was she going to tell him the truth, that she'd never really loved him?

"Well?"

Oh, Mom remained at the door.

Ronnie shrugged. "Gavin."

"Hmm."

Yeah, hmmm. She held up the letter. "Mind if I have some privacy?"

"It's your house."

Could have fooled me.

Yikes, she really, really needed Mom to move out.

After Mom closed the door, Ronnie tucked pillows behind her back, propped herself against them, and opened the letter.

My dear Veronica,

His *dear* Veronica?

I met a couple this week. She came to me for concussion treatment, and he accompanied her. While I talked with them, they ended up sharing their story.

What was it that made patients spill their life story to Gavin?

They're a little older than you and me. She had been in the military. He was a civilian working a high-paying white-collar job. During her enlistment, their marriage fell apart and they eventually divorced. I guess that's common in military families. But over the years, neither remarried. Then one day, they bumped into each other. Literally. Hence the concussion.

It was then they realized how selfish their separation had been.

Selfish? Wait, was Gavin calling her selfish?
Well, wasn't she?
Oh, if only she could make her conscience shut up.

And lazy.

He did not just call her lazy! Dearest Gavin, this was not the way to win her back.

You see, both worked extra hard at their jobs to be the best they could be, and they succeeded, but when they came home, they got lazy, and didn't give their all to their marriage.

She and Gavin had only been married a day and a half before her world caved in, and they'd definitely given their all in that snippet of time. What was his point?

But when they "bumped" into each other, it was as if Someone had knocked sense into their heads. They missed each other. And now they've vowed to work hard and make their courtship and marriage a priority. You never know what methods God might choose to bring people together.

Oh, she knew what he was doing. His stories always had a purpose, and this one was an enticement to bring them back together.

I guess what I'm trying to say is that I'm sorry for placing work above our relationship. Yes, I've had the excuse that healing brains is an important job, but caring for those closest in our lives—you!—is more important. I was lazy and did not give my all to our relationship. If I had, I'm certain we'd have married sooner.

And now because of my indolence, I have a hole in my heart where you should be. This house echoes with emptiness.

I miss you. I miss Jelly Bean.

There's an old proverb that says, "Absence makes the heart grow fonder." I can verify that is true. I pray that you will choose to return home soon, and I vow to place our relationship above my career.

With all my love,
Gavin

Ronnie sniffled, but forbid any tears. Gavin was a good man, and she didn't deserve him. The sooner she told him that, the quicker he could move on. She picked up her phone and called him, holding her breath as it rang through to voice mail. No doubt he was at church. Where she should be, but she no longer had a church home.

She left a pithy message, one he'd appreciate. "Gavin, we need to talk."

Chapter Eight

Not planning to go to church, Ronnie dressed for a jog so she could get out of her apartment and have some time to herself. She'd whip up a protein drink then head on out.

Mom sat on the couch, immersed in a book. How odd not to see Mom preparing for church. She always dressed and looked her best, and had encouraged Ronnie to do the same. If not for Dad's selfishness...

How true Gavin's letter was. If Dad had given more of himself to Mom, none of them would be in this predicament. When it came to his marriage, he had been lazy.

"Going somewhere?" Mom looked up from her book.

"Out for a jog. Do you mind watching Evie?"

"Not at all."

The expected answer, of course. This was one advantage of having Mom here. But when Ronnie returned home from her jog, she wanted her little girl all to herself for the day.

She removed her smoothie blender from the pantry. She put in a cup of frozen berries, added protein powder and flax seeds, a touch of honey to sweeten it, and a half cup of almond milk. That should give her plenty of protein to begin the day. After blending it, she sipped in between stretches.

"What are your plans for the day?" Ronnie asked, hoping Mom would say she was getting together with friends or going shopping.

"I was thinking of taking Evie to Como Park. You said she enjoyed the zoo last Sunday."

Ronnie froze mid-stretch, then slowly stood straight, fighting the urge to be combative. "Actually, I have a day planned for just Evie and me. Why don't you meet some friends for coffee?"

Mom set her book down, her lips a grim line. "I told Evie last night I was taking her to the zoo. She'll be very upset if we don't go."

And I'll be upset if you do.

"You should have run it by me first. She is *my* daughter."

Mom looked to the floor, clearly upset, but Ronnie couldn't help that. Evie was her daughter, and this was her home. She would not let Mom take over.

"Do you know how many so-called friends have called me since this...this incident?"

Ronnie sighed. "Let me guess, they've all canceled you."

"Canceled?"

"Um." How to explain this current-day slang? "It means withdrawing support and attention from you."

Mom stood and gazed out the window at the parkland behind the apartment. "Then it appears I have been canceled by extension of being your father's wife."

"I'm sorry." Ronnie joined her mom at the window. She hadn't heard from any so-called True North friends either, but all those relationships had been superficial. They weren't a big loss for her, but for Mom, her church relationships had been her existence. "It stinks."

"Like rotten milk."

"Uh-uh. Like Evie's diapers."

"Yes. Like that." Mom leaned into her shoulder. "I don't know where I belong anymore. I don't know who I am without the church or your father. They swallowed me up years ago, and now I've been vomited out like Jonah."

"So, there's no chance of you and Dad getting back together?"

"Ha! Did you know he thought he could return to True North? Thought all would be forgiven if he stood up and gave a sermon about forgiving seventy times seven? I'm not the only one who's been swallowed up. He never used to be that way."

"Then I guess we'll just have to give you a fresh start." Which was what they all needed, but for Mom, Ronnie planned to jumpstart her parents' marriage. They'd hit the bottom, now it was time to start clawing their way back up. Mom may not think, right now, that her marriage had a future, but Ronnie was determined to convince her otherwise because a) Ronnie needed her place back and b) parents belonged together. Period.

She linked her arm with her mom's and led her to her bedroom. Opened the closet. "First thing is, you have to get rid of these grannie clothes. Yes, you're a grandma, but you don't have to look it."

"I like my clothes."

"I'm sure you do, but you can do better."

Mom harumphed, which Ronnie ignored and led her to the guest bath mirror.

"And you've worn this hairstyle since you got married."

"Because I like it."

"I'm sure you do, but it ages you twenty years. Time for an upgrade."

Mom spun around and wagged a finger. "You're scheming something."

"Yes, I am. If you want a life, then we need to drag you into the twenty-first century."

Mom turned back to the mirror and played with her hair. "You're not talking a new romance, I hope. I don't plan to revisit that ever again."

"Nope. Not a new romance." Just an old one. "How about we start today? All three of us Whitmer women deserve to have a day of shopping therapy."

"Ending with ice cream?"

"Absolutely." When Ronnie was young, their shopping days always were topped off with ice cream. "It's time to introduce Evie to this important tradition."

And it was time to begin Operation: Matchmaker. If Dad could play matchmaker, so could she. Step One involved updating Mom's look—Dad wouldn't be able to resist her. Step Two would commence whenever Gavin called back. Step Three would be the most difficult: Meet up with her father and try not to strangle him.

Laughter followed Ronnie into her apartment. She couldn't remember having such a fun, carefree day with Mom. They'd all become too stiff. But now, Mom had an up-to-date wardrobe, and sometime this week, if Ronnie could make an appointment, Mom's 1980s big hair would be banished forever. Her plan was in motion.

Despite Evie's temporary sugar high after eating ice cream, she now struggled to keep her eyelids open. But if any of them wanted sleep tonight, Evie couldn't go to sleep for another hour. This would not be a fun hour.

She placed Evie's diaper bag in the nursery and came out to see Mom and granddaughter on the floor together, making animal noises with Evie's stuffed friends. She tugged her phone from her pocket and discretely filmed the two for several seconds. Someday they'd all look back on this time and see that not every moment was cloudy.

Her phone rang as she was recording. Gavin. She quickly ended the video and answered.

"Hey."

"Veronica."

It was as if they were back to that awkward first-date stage. And with Gavin, who spoke so little, it had been even worse.

"You needed to talk?" Gavin sounded hopeful.

She hated dousing it, and wouldn't do so with Mom in the room. "Um, I did. Can you hold a second?"

"Sure."

She covered the mic and looked to her mom, who was watching intently. "Do you mind if—"

"Go." She waved her hand. "Evie and I are having fun."

Huh, someone else was playing matchmaker, but she was fully aware of what Mom was scheming and would be ready. "I'm going to take this out in the hall. Thanks for watching Evie."

"Never a problem."

She uncovered the mic to speak with Gavin and aimed for the front door. "I'm back and heading outside so we can talk."

"Your mother's with you?"

Ronnie laughed and shut the door behind her. "Moved in a week ago, hence this phone call today, but first I need to thank you for the flowers. They're lovely."

"They mean I miss you."

Of course they did.

"Well, I appreciate them and your note and your stories."

"Appreciate..."

Yeah, probably not the word he wanted to hear. "Do you mind if we, uh, can we meet up somewhere? Are you busy tonight?"

"Not too busy for you."

Just like his note said.

"How about Gina's Café in Amery?"

"I can be there in ten minutes."

"Make it thirty."

"Sure."

So, thirty short minutes until she broke his heart.

Ronnie changed into something stylish and refreshed her makeup but didn't quite know why. She didn't need to make a good impression anymore. After all, he was her husband.

Then twenty minutes later she strode into Gina's, a cute independent café that served organic food fresh from local farmers. But that wasn't the main reason why she chose this place. The booths had high backs and therefore plenty of privacy. This kind of talk needed to be private.

She found Gavin already seated, water poured, and fresh rolls placed in the center of the table. Naturally, he was ready for her. Same old Gavin.

But he didn't look the same. Contacts instead of glasses. A beard that intentionally gave the impression of a five o'clock shadow, and it looked mighty nice on him. He'd even combed his hair differently. Less *Father Knows Best* and more Zac Efron. Was he attempting to impress her? She couldn't deny that this look worked for him.

He stood as she neared, always the gentleman, and didn't sit until she was comfortable.

"You're looking well." She sipped at her water and eyed him over her glass.

He rubbed a hand over his beard. "Not sure I like it."

"Oh, but I do." The true yet careless words slipped out. The last thing she wanted to do was give him hope for their marriage.

Still, his eyes lit up. "You look nice, too."

She shrugged. "Thanks."

"Are you ready to order?" A waiter had snuck up on them.

Ronnie hadn't looked at the menu but didn't really need to. "I'm ready. You?" She looked at Gavin.

"Go ahead."

"I'll have your butternut squash salad."

"And I'll take your top sirloin, please."

"Coming right up."

The server left, returning their privacy.

"Anyway." Ronnie rotated her water glass between her hands. "Thanks for meeting me on short notice."

"Always, Veronica."

"Would you stop being so nice?"

He winced as if slapped.

"I'm sorry, it's just that..." She sighed and took a drink of water. "This is hard for me to say because I like you."

"Like."

So, he caught that. Duh, of course he did.

She wiped her mouth with a napkin and kept the napkin close to her lips. "There's not a delicate way to say this, but our wedding was a mistake."

He said nothing, but the way his cheeks tightened, he was probably gritting his teeth.

"It's not your fault. It's...it's that I was attracted to...I loved a status symbol, and that's not fair to you."

"What are you saying?"

Oh, he knew what she was telling him. He was

sometimes clueless in matters of romance, but he wasn't that naïve. Clearly, he wanted her to say the words.

"We should get a divorce."

His fists clenched on the table. "No."

"No?" This wasn't going at all how she'd planned. She was supposed to bring up the Operation: Matchmaker first. Now she'd botched that, too.

"Marriage isn't something I take lightly."

"Oh, so that's why you pushed me for a spur-of-the-moment wedding."

"And I've apologized for that."

"But the fact remains that it shouldn't have happened. You deserve someone who loves you wholly, not just your degrees."

He laughed, shaking his head. "The answer's still no."

"I don't need your approval to file."

"But you do need my signature, I believe."

"Why are you being so stubborn?"

He leaned toward her, and she got a whiff of aftershave. He never wore aftershave. "Because you're being impulsive."

"I..." Yeah, she was, but that didn't mean she was wrong.

Actually...She sat up straight as an idea came to her. This might just work out better than she'd planned.

"Okay, I agree that I'm being impulsive, just as getting married was."

He nodded, giving her that point.

"So I have a proposal for you."

His mouth crooked up to the right. "Proposal, huh?"

"Mom's driving me crazy. She moved in without being invited. She's constantly telling me how to care for Evie. I'm a grownup being treated like a child. I need her to move back home with Dad."

"She has every right to be angry with him."

"But ending their forty-year marriage without even trying to reconcile? Dad and Mom preached forgiveness all the time. That preaching is being tested for the first time, and Mom is failing."

He sighed and took a drink of water, his gaze wandering the restaurant before returning to her. "What's your proposal?"

"A Bible study?"

His brows shot up faster than a rocket. "Excuse me?"

"That's how they first met, where they fell in love. I found a seven-week program that I know will bring them back together."

"And if it doesn't?"

"I'll have given it my best shot."

"And you need me to be involved?"

She grinned. "To protect Dad from me and Mom."

At that he laughed. "Point taken."

"Besides, Dad likes you."

"Like his daughter, he likes my credentials."

Direct hit to the conscience, but that wasn't going to stop her. "Are you game?"

"A Bible study is never a bad idea."

"Good."

"But just so you realize, that also gives me seven weeks

to win your heart back.”

“Hmm. Is that a threat?”

“Dearest Veronica, that is a promise.”

Chapter Nine

"I still can't believe you talked me into this Bible study with your father." Mom primped in the mirror, running her fingers through her stylish new hairdo. Dad's eyes were going to bug out when he saw Mom. With the wardrobe and hair makeover, on top of the pounds she was shedding under the stress of the situation, she'd dropped twenty years.

"It's a condition of you living rent-free with me." That was the only way she could think of to get her mom to agree. Gavin had worked on Dad, who apparently was in rough shape.

Served him right for what he'd done.

But in spite of her anger toward him, she still did love him. He was her father after all. His awful actions had cost him everything. His job, his wife, daughter, reputation.

But if God could forgive a minister for messing up His church, she could forgive a father who wanted the best for his daughter, even if he went about it in a completely wrong way.

There was a knock on her door, so Ronnie looked at the

time. Six PM. Their sitter, a responsible teen who lived in her building, was certainly punctual. Evie would be thrilled to see her friend again.

"Hey, baby girl." Ronnie stepped into the nursery where Evie sat playing in a cardboard box, of all things. "Latasha's here to play with you."

"I pway!" She clapped her hands then raised her arms to be lifted from the box.

Five minutes later, Ronnie and her mom were in her Prius heading for Gavin's home, a neutral location for her parents, if not for her. Gavin wasn't playing fair, insisting it be at his mansion-like home. He'd said he wasn't a fan of it, but it was a connection to his Arizona-snowbird parents who'd passed along the home to him, so he stayed. And she'd encouraged him to stay because she was in awe. Now, she wished he'd find another smaller home she wouldn't be covetous of.

They arrived at his house too quickly. Bibles in hand, Ronnie walked with her mom over the cobblestone sidewalk to the front door. Should she ring the bell? For months she'd just walked on in as if it were her own home, but she'd lost that right.

She pushed the button, and moments later Gavin opened the door with a scowl.

"You can just come on in. This is your home."

"I..." She shut her mouth as arguing would be pointless. Mr. Logical always seemed to win. "Next week."

"I'll hold you to it. You ring the bell, I don't open the door."

"Then I leave."

"Touché." He gestured for them to come in. "Pastor Whitmer's in my study."

"You realize, his days as a pastor are probably over," Ronnie said to Gavin while gesturing for Mom to enter first.

"Maybe within physical church walls. I have a feeling God is just beginning to use him."

"We'll see."

"Oh, ye of little faith." He grinned. Amazing how that new beard of his made his grin much more enchanting.

He let Ronnie take the lead to the study, a room Belle from *Beauty and the Beast* would be envious of. Bookshelves lined every wall from floor to a very high ceiling. A floating ladder had to be used to reach the top shelves.

"Baby girl." Dad stood when she entered the room.

Gavin hadn't been kidding when he'd said her dad looked rough. His clothes hung loose on his frame, his hair needed a trim, and his beard was scraggly.

She refrained from asking, "How are you?" What she saw answered that question too clearly. She also refused to say it was good to see him. About that, she was still uncertain.

"Dad." She nodded and ignored his open arms as she chose a chair opposite him.

He sat and his shoulders drooped as if unseen hands were pushing down on them. Perhaps they were. Demons were real, weren't they? And Dad obviously had his.

But then his eyes lit up and widened when Mom walked in the room. Just the impact she'd hoped for.

"Cheryl, you came."

She huffed. "Not like I had much choice. It was come here or be homeless." Her gaze shot darts at Ronnie.

"Well, now that we're all comfortable." Gavin gave a sideways glance to Ronnie then handed her four side-stapled booklets. "Would you care to facilitate the discussion?"

"I suppose." Since she was the one who came up with the idea and created the study, that made sense, though Gavin would do a much better job. Funny how he'd been a Christian only a few years and already knew the Bible far better than she did.

She handed a booklet to each and sat, suddenly nervous about teaching a Bible study to a pastor and his wife and a neurologist. As a lukewarm Christian, she was definitely not the person to be teaching, but if this brought her parents together again, it was worth the effort.

"So..." She cleared her scratchy throat. "A few Sundays back I visited Kyle's church in Northfield. His pastor was kind enough to stop and chat with me, but then he gave me an assignment. I'm just sharing the love."

"What's his name?" Dad asked. "I might know him."

She shrugged. "Pastor Mitch is all I know. He preaches at New Hope."

Dad shook his head. The church was undoubtedly too small for Dad to have taken notice.

"Now tonight is—"

"Veronica, may I say something?" Dad leaned toward her.

Why was she "Veronica" all of a sudden?

Regardless, she nodded, but was prepared to stop him if he talked too long. Like any self-respecting pastor, he could talk on and on for an entire hour without taking a breath. Or so it seemed.

He folded his hands together, remained silent for a moment, then looked at the small group, connecting momentarily with each of them. "I'm sorry." He bowed his head again.

Wait. That was it? No grand soliloquy?

"For what?" Uh-oh, now Mom was on the loose. Lately, that wasn't good. "For ruining our marriage, the church, your daughter's marriage? Sentencing your innocent granddaughter to a life shuttled between two houses. Two little words are hardly enough."

He coughed and his shoulders hunched even more. She'd always thought him a large man who could look very intimidating, but he suddenly appeared small and frail.

"You're right, Cheryl." His hands squeezed together. "I've thrown away everything good. Even when I called Veronica earlier, I had hopes that True North would welcome me back." He shook his head. "When I've quoted Micah 6:8, my finger has always been pointed at the congregation. I didn't fathom that God was trying to speak to me."

Silence took over and Ronnie counted ten beats of the grandfather clock poised in the corner of the room before retaking the lead.

"Well, I guess that's a good place for us to begin." She

shuffled the booklet and Bible in her lap. "When I went to Kyle's new church, I was looking for truth because to me, everything in my life had been a lie. Pastor Mitch didn't tell me straight out, but rather gave me an assignment. I thought it was arrogant and threw away what he'd written down. Somehow, his words stayed in my head, so I'm guessing there's a reason for it. Since we've all been affected by"— she looked down, not wanting to make eye contact with her father—"Dad's actions, I figured maybe we could all learn from this."

She heard shuffling feet and throats clearing, but no one interrupted.

"My goal over these next seven weeks, not counting today, is to explore what Pastor Mitch called the seven 'I Am' statements."

"Ahhh," came from her dad, but that was all. He was doing far better at staying quiet than she'd anticipated.

"But tonight, to begin, I want to look at another verse the pastor recommended. John 1:1-5. I'll read it out loud."

She stumbled through the pages of her Bible to find John, reciting Matthew, Mark, Luke, and John in her head. If she'd have been smart, she would have looked up the verses earlier, read through them, underlined and bookmarked her Bible. Lesson learned for next week.

She finally found the verses and read them aloud, twice, trying to ascertain the meaning. "Anyone care to talk about these verses?" She sure didn't understand how it related to the "I Am" statements.

Surprisingly, neither Dad nor Mom leaped in to discuss.

So far, they were behaving very well.

"What are your thoughts, Veronica?"

Oh, sure, Gavin had to put her on the spot. She'd look like a fool in front of the pastor and the genius.

She read it again. "Well, it sounds to me like John's talking about Jesus. That he's eternal." She tapped her Bible. "And these are His words."

His words. Ah, now it was making sense. Before she could believe the "I Am" statements, she had to understand that Jesus and the Word were synonymous.

"I couldn't have said it better." High praise from Dad.

"Really?" She looked to him like a little girl seeking approval from her father.

He seemed to sit up straighter, taller, and nodded.

That was all she needed to keep going and to go over the assignment for next week. Mom said little during the entire time, but that wasn't a surprise. She wasn't happy to be here, so she was sulking like a small child. Hopefully, that would soon change, and sometime over the next seven weeks, Mom and Dad would be riding in the same vehicle—she hoped—which would mean that Mom had moved back home.

Now that was a glorious thought.

"Daydreaming?" Gavin's light touch on her arm startled her.

"Yep." She made a slight hand gesture toward her parents and he nodded in understanding. At least they were on the same page when it came to her parents. Maybe if she and Gavin gave them some time alone, they'd open up to each other.

"Can I speak to you for a minute?" She nodded toward the door, hoping he'd get the hint that she wanted to talk to him alone.

"Sure. You left something here you might want."

Not a surprise, given the speed in which she'd left that awful day a few weeks back.

Without saying anything, she got up and followed Gavin into a hall decorated with gilded-frame portraits. Gavin's parents, grandparents, great-grandparents. All who'd lived in this home before him. Many of them had been blessed with the genius gene. Chances were, if she and Gavin had stayed together, if they'd had a child, the child would be brilliant. She wasn't a dummy, but genius? Far from it.

"Admiring the creepy wall?" Suddenly he was beside her, occupying too much of her space with his presence.

"You think it's creepy?"

"Don't you?"

"Yeah, well, they're your family."

"They are, and I'm grateful for them, but this wall has always struck me as stuffy. I was hoping you'd help me redecorate."

"You'd let me?"

"When you move back in, yes."

Ah, of course, a caveat, to which she didn't reply.

Instead, he handed her a white gift bag, filling the silence. "Thought you might miss this."

She peeked inside, then up at Gavin. No surprise, he was blushing. She pulled her barely-there wedding-night lingerie from the bag and got the expected result as his face turned fire-engine red.

Problem was, with his new glasses-free look and the blush, the man looked downright sexy. And the way his gaze swept from her eyes to her lips made her weak in the knees. He touched her cheek with the slightest caress, stealing her breath.

His hooded gaze met hers. "May I kiss you?"

Her mouth opened, but couldn't force the word, "No." Instead, she nodded, dropping her chemise on the hardwood.

His lips brushed over hers like angel wings, stealing her resolve.

But he broke away, just as she planned to go deeper, leaving her standing on legs made of jelly. He gripped her arms, giving her balance, and rested his forehead against hers. "I wouldn't complain if you stayed the night. After all, you are my wi—"

"Get out of my sight!"

Mom's screech knifed through their moment and they both hurried into the library.

Mom stood across the room from Dad, her arm arrow-straight toward the door while he cowered in his chair. Two weeks ago, Ronnie wouldn't have believed such a sight to be possible.

"What's going on?" She cuffed her hands on her hips, feeling felt like the parent here, not the daughter.

"Your...that man...he's ruined our lives, and I can't play nice anymore. I can't make small talk and pretend nothing's wrong. It's time for us to go home."

Home? Ronnie's place was *not* her mother's home. As much as she wanted to add that point to her argument, she held her tongue and gestured toward the front door.

"Let's go."

"About time." Mom grabbed her purse and stalked from the room.

Ronnie mouthed, "I'm sorry" to Gavin. In more ways than one. When he'd asked her to stay the night, she'd been more than willing to say "Yes." Couldn't wait to send her parents out the door so she could spend a passionate night with her husband.

And give him the wrong idea. Break his heart all over again. She couldn't do that to him.

Gavin invited her dad to stay a few minutes, then walked Mom and her out to the car. His hand grazed her arm before she got in. She knew better than to look up into his eyes tonight as she'd likely give in.

"You forgot this again." He handed her the gift bag with her chemise. "Know that I'll miss you and I'm praying for you."

At that, she risked looking up at him. One would think that growing up a daughter of a pastor, she'd have heard those words—"praying for you"—often. When they had been spoken, there'd been a lack of authenticity behind them, but when Gavin said those words, she knew he meant them.

"Thank you," she whispered.

And he pressed a kiss to her forehead. "Text me when

you get home."

She nodded and quietly settled into the driver's seat.

He closed her door and stepped back.

His gaze remained on her as she started the car, then drove it down the long, tree-lined drive. She was sure he watched her as she felt the tingle up her spine until she turned onto the county road removing her car from his sight.

The tingle was replaced by a painful numbness that made no sense. She hadn't felt like this around him before they married. Why now?

Probably just because he was forbidden, and that was always attractive to her. Truth was, Gavin deserved better.

Chapter Ten

lowers again."

Ronnie glared at her mom, who still hadn't learned to knock on her bedroom door before entering. But her glare was softened by the colorful bouquet with a variety of flowers. It had arrived just in time to replace the now-wilting carnations from a week ago.

"It appears as if someone is trying to woo you?"

"Woo?" She chuckled and sat up in bed. "Yes, he might be trying to romance me." The thought made her smile inside and out, which, in turn, irritated her.

"Well, just remember to keep your guard up. You can't trust men."

And that made her stomach and fists clench. "Just because you couldn't trust Dad, doesn't mean all men are like that. Gavin doesn't have an inauthentic bone in his body." Exactly the opposite of her.

She got out of bed and took the arrangement with a disingenuous "thank you," then whisked her mom out the door. Mom was definitely right about one thing: Gavin was trying to woo her, and that thought made every hummingbird in her stomach take flight as she placed the flowers on her windowsill.

Maybe a romantic evening wouldn't be such a bad idea. After all, they were married, so Gavin would have no guilt.

She removed the card and brought it back to her bed. Before ripping open the envelope, she fluffed the pillows behind her, making them as comfy as possible. At last, she tore the envelope and took out the card. A sunrise—or was it a sunset?—was pictured on the front, unbroken by words. Inside, along with the letter she'd come to expect, he'd written, *Know that I love you, Gavin.*

There went those hummingbirds again. She didn't try to stifle her grin as she unfolded the letter and began reading.

> *Dearest Veronica,*
>
> *A couple I know recently broke up. They'd lived together a number of years before this happened, had become parents during the interim. Yet, their relationship didn't survive. When speaking with my friend, he admitted that their love for each other had diminished over time, that in the end, the relationship was little more than sex, which was how it began as well. It grieved him that a child was involved, but he refused to subject their son to their apathy. He claimed they never even fought, but came to be two strangers living in the same home.*
>
> *Research has shown that marriage begun by*

couples living together prior to the wedding have a much greater chance of ending in divorce. Sex is a very weak thread when that alone ties a couple together.

And, as your parents have learned, a cord of three strands is the strongest. When they abandoned God, their relationship was easily broken.

Which leads me to my behavior this past Wednesday. I admit, I was overwhelmed by being near you again, and let my emotions get the best of me. That will not happen again. I promise. I cherish you too much.

I realize now that my feelings are not returned. Before our marriage, I was blinded to that or perhaps I simple chose not to see it. It pains me to admit that I allowed your father's endorsement of our marriage to speak louder than God's voice. Had I prayed for direction rather than walking the easy path, you and I would not be in this predicament. For that I am dearly sorry.

I feel as if that is a common theme of my letters.

Know this, dearest Veronica, I will continue to pursue you. Though we no longer share the same home, the same bed, my heart is tethered to yours. When I vowed to love, honor, and cherish you through sickness and in health, I

meant those words and will abide by them.
With all my heart,
Gavin

Ronnie clutched the letter against her heart that was beating to an erratic rhythm. Every emotion possible had passed through her as she read the letter—hope, anger, sadness—ending with one she couldn't define. Those first few lines of the letter, he could have been describing her and Kyle.

Until lately, she hadn't realized how selfish her actions toward Kyle had been. Now their relationship was irreparably broken, and they'd dragged a child into their brokenness.

Gavin was right, which wasn't a shock.

The hummingbirds resumed their fluttering. Yes, Gavin was right. Their wedding had happened based on selfishness and lies. Much like her relationship with Kyle. Just like her parents' marriage.

Huh. Her boss's words, imploring Ronnie to explore what "truth" was, flitted through her mind. That combined with Pastor Mitch's "I Am" assignment had her realizing that unlike opinion, truth wasn't subjective and different for each person.

If she wanted Evie to have a better future, it was time to let truth win.

That didn't start with romancing Gavin, but rather, learning who "I Am" really was. Which meant it was time to dig into her Bible, so she'd be prepared to lead the discussion this Wednesday. She prayed it would be an eye opener for all of them.

Ronnie had written "I Am the bread of life" on her notepad, the first of the "I Am" statements. She shifted her Bible and notes on her lap, her nerves getting the better of her in Gavin's library, electrified by the tension emanating from her parents. Mom hadn't budged one bit in her attitude. And Dad? Well, the mousy man from last week had disappeared, and had been replaced by someone curious.

As long as that man wasn't soon replaced by the arrogant person he'd become before he fell.

She cleared her throat to get everyone's attention. "Who would like to read John six?"

After a moment, Gavin volunteered and began reading. The specific "I Am" references were mid-chapter but, thanks to wisdom from Gavin, she'd started reading the entire chapter to understand the context. Made her realize how often she'd spouted a single verse to make a point, when the context would have proven something else altogether.

How had someone who'd only been a believer for three years become wiser than those who'd believed their entire lives?

She studied Gavin as he read. The man was so earnest in

his belief and read the passage with a true passion, unlike the made-up-for-stage passion displayed by her father for so many years. How had she not seen that before? She supposed that when a person had a single focus, they could zoom in on the detail they wanted to see and ignore the rest.

When he finished reading, Gavin kept his head low. Praying?

Praying!

Oh my, she hadn't even thought to open the evening with prayer, and doing so now would be as fake as she'd feel saying those prayers. Gavin had been too kind to call her on it. Instead he covered them all without drawing attention to himself.

Following the reading, she led a discussion for several minutes. Mom did a lot of grunting, Dad a lot of nodding, with Gavin often expounding on his thoughts. She then invited him to pray, which he did from his heart and not to prove how loquacious or how close to God he was. No doubt, he had no clue how attractive that was. What would he say if she asked him out?

"Ronnie, what do you say about that?"

What? She shook her head and looked to her dad, mortified that she'd been caught daydreaming about Gavin when she was supposed to be leading a Bible study.

She gulped, trying to look composed. "Could you repeat your question?"

"Would you mind if I led the study in two weeks?"

Mom did more grunting and Ronnie's radar zoomed up. Wasn't she leading well enough? Did he think he could do better?

"I—"

He raised his hands. "Sorry, I should offer an explanation."

"Okay." This should be good.

He clutched his Bible, his gaze focused on it. "The third statement is 'I am the door of the sheep.' As a former shepherd, I have some new insights on that statement that aren't at all complimentary to me. I'd like to study it further."

She blinked, digesting what he'd said. "Yes. Of course."

Actually, maybe if each of them would lead a week, the study would become more personal.

"Mom, is there a week you'd like to take?"

Her now gaunt cheeks hollowed even more. "I'd prefer to soak it in."

"That's fine."

"Veronica." Gavin grabbed her attention with his gentle delivery of her name. "I'd be glad to lead next week."

"I'd like that."

He smiled and her heart danced a waltz.

She had to look away and focus on the task at hand. "After week three, we'll decide who wants to lead."

"Time to go?" Mom got up faster than Ronnie had seen her move in years.

"I was hoping to have a moment to speak with Gavin in private."

"I'll see you in the car."

Okay, then. So, Mom wasn't even going to try. She

glanced over at Dad, whose gaze was riveted on the library doorway. "I don't think she'll ever forgive me."

"It's only been a month, Pastor." Gavin spoke her father's title with too-much reverence, in Ronnie's opinion. "She needs time for her heart to mend."

"I suppose." Dad breathed out. "And please just call me Dean. My shepherding days are over.

"Or maybe they're just beginning." The hope-filled words came without thought from Ronnie. But she meant them. "Maybe you'll be shepherding a different kind of flock."

Dad nodded. "Something to think on. Pray on." He shook Gavin's hand. "Thank you, son, for hosting again. I look forward to next week." His gaze shot to Ronnie. "And please don't give up on my daughter. I've made a lot of mistakes with her, but you're not one of them."

Dad peered down at her, his gaze softer than she ever recalled. "I love you, Ronnie." He turned and left without trying to hug her, respecting her space. Could it be he was really becoming a new man?

"We've been meeting." Gavin gestured to a chair. "Do you have a minute?"

She grinned, happy to spend alone time with Gavin, and a little too pleased about making Mom wait out in the car. "Of course."

"You got my note?" He sat opposite her.

"And the flowers. They're lovely. Thank you."

"Then you comprehend where I stand on our relationship."

"I do." She leaned toward him. "But I also want you to know that it's working."

He looked genuinely confused. "What's working?"

"You'll see." She winked and got up.

"Sometimes I fear I'll never understand the opposite sex." He walked alongside her, heading out of the library and toward the front door.

They reached the door and she stopped, keeping an appropriate distance between them. "Dr. Coborn, I think you understand us just fine. Just keep doing what you're doing."

"Well." He scratched the back of his head, mussing his hair. "I have a confession. I've had a little help with all this." He motioned from his new hair style to his updated wardrobe.

Not a surprise, really. A nerd doesn't change into a model without some help.

"Angie's been giving me some advice."

"Well, you can tell your nurse practitioner to keep up the good work. I approve."

He smiled at that. "Does that mean you're willing to work on our relationship?"

"It means." She cupped her hand around the doorknob. "That I would like to ask you out on a date."

This time he grinned. "You would?"

"You available Saturday?"

"Hmm." He checked his phone. "Looks like I've got a date."

"What?"

"Got ya." He laughed. "A date. With you."

"Funny guy." She pretend-socked him on the arm, amused by this rare comedic side of Gavin. "Then I guess I'll see you early Saturday morning. And wear jeans."

Chapter Eleven

Ronnie stood in the doorway of her walk-in closet, her gaze roving over her clothes. Yes, today's date was a jeans and T-shirt event, but she had to choose the correct jeans and shirt and shoes to make the best impression. Realistically, she didn't have to make an impression, but today's date was different from past ones. For some reason, today felt like she was going on her first date with Gavin, all over again, and she was giddy with anticipation.

She finally settled on skinny jeans, a mauve tank, and a button-down shirt just in case it got chilly. Her hiking boots would work well with the outfit. She got dressed, wrapped her hair in a messy bun and got approval from her mirror.

But that wasn't the opinion that mattered most.

Butterflies flitted through her stomach at the image of Gavin in jeans.

Oh for Pete's sake, he was her husband, not a high school crush. But she sure couldn't convince her nerves of that.

She made one last check in the mirror before heading out to the living room where Mom sat on the floor with Evie.

They did play well together, and Ronnie appreciated all the time Mom spent babysitting for free.

Still.

She cleared her throat to grab their attention. "What do you think?"

"You're wearing that on a date with Gavin?"

"We're going hiking. What am I supposed to wear?"

"I suppose. I just wouldn't have chosen hiking."

"Guess it wasn't up to you."

Mom shrugged, conceding the point. "If your date goes well, you just might be moving back in with your husband, and I can stay here."

And who would pay the rent? Ronnie wanted to ask but clamped her mouth shut to avoid another argument.

The doorbell rang, saving her blood pressure from going sky high. This living situation had gone on far too long.

"I get it." Evie raced Ronnie to the door, the little stinker.

Ronnie crossed a leg in front of her daughter before opening the door. Pretty soon, the child was going to zoom out quicker than Ronnie could stop her.

"Dada Gabin!"

"Hey, Jelly Bean." He bent down and opened his arms, and she leaped into them, knocking him on his behind. "So you've missed me?"

She nodded and covered his face with kisses.

"I missed you, too." Keeping her in his arm, he stood and grinned at Ronnie. "You look nice."

"I could say the same for you." Yeah, he wore his jeans and plain shirt very nicely, indeed. "Did you have help getting dressed?"

"Huh. I feel as if I've been insulted." He planted a kiss on Evie's cheek. "For your information, I chose this outfit all by myself."

"Bravo. You did well."

"Thank you."

"Are you two lovebirds going to leave?" Mom tried to sound annoyed, but amusement came through her voice. "Or are you going to stand in the doorway and flirt all day?"

Was that what they were doing?

Gavin's bashful shrug gave her the answer.

Which made her not want to waste another moment of the day. She latched her hands around Evie's waist. "Say goodbye to Dada Gavin."

"Bye-bye Dada." Evie slobbered another kiss on his cheek before Ronnie could snatch her away.

"Sorry about that." Ronnie handed Evie over to her mom before grabbing a tissue and wiping Evie-goobies from Gavin's face.

He shrugged. "Could be worse things than getting kisses from my stepdaughter."

His stepdaughter. Did that mean they were closer to getting back together? Maybe today would solidify their relationship. Maybe after today she would be moving back in with Gavin, and Mom could keep this place. Temporarily.

She prayed so, as she practically shoved him out the door and sighed once the door clicked shut behind her.

"Rough morning?"

"Mom's rubbing me the wrong way. I feel like I'm a small child around her, and it's all I can do to keep from talking back."

"I might have an answer for that arrangement."

"Oh really?" Was that a hint that she was going to be invited back home?

"We'll talk about it in the car. You said it'll be a bit of a drive."

"About three and a half hours."

"Then we'll need something to talk about, besides you telling me where we're going."

"Don't you like a little mystery?"

"The brain is mystery enough."

Spoken like a true brain doctor.

Moments later, they were in his Mercedes and heading north out of the cities.

"Now you'll tell me where we're going?" He shot a quick glance in her direction.

"Well." She kicked off her boots and reclined in her seat. "I wanted something different from what we usually did."

"You didn't like orchestral concerts and theatrical shows?"

"Oh, I did." She slapped a hand to her heart. "Preceded by a fancy meal. You spoiled me."

"But...?" Vehicles whooshed past them in the left-hand lane, not appreciating the follow-the-rules-of-the-road driver.

"I got to thinking that we had little time to talk on those dates."

He shrugged. "Maybe that was the plan."

Spoken like a true introvert who also tended to be on the shy side. "And maybe that was our problem to begin with."

He drummed his fingers on the steering while for a minute before saying, "Because we didn't really know each other."

"Exactly. So, I planned a date with a long car ride—"

"Where to?"

"I'm getting to that." He may not like mysteries, but she sure liked teasing him with one. "We have to talk. And when we're hiking—"

"Hiking?"

"Mm-hmm. We'll have more time to talk."

"Or maybe you'll do the talking, and I'll do the listening."

"Nope. Won't let that happen."

He drummed his fingers again, and she mimicked him, playing to the beat of some unknown tune on her thighs.

"So, what's your plan to get Mom out of my apartment?"

"Uh-uh. No changing the subject."

"It was worth a try."

He turned on his blinker. All she saw up ahead was a fast-food joint.

"Tell me where we're going, or we're feasting on fast-food burgers."

"Sounds like a threat." She grinned in his direction.

He aimed for the turn lane.

"Okay, fine. I'll tell you."

He swerved back onto the road and was greeted with honking horns. She resisted a not-so-nice return action.

"I was trying to think where a neurologist would enjoy spending time, and I figured the Mississippi headwaters was the perfect place. Get it? Brain? Head?" She giggled at her own lame joke.

He merely shook his head. "You're funny."

"But seriously, have you ever been there? It's beautiful."

"Actually." He scratched his whiskers. "I haven't been."

"Perfect. So when you walk across the Mississippi for the first time, I get to be there."

"You'll hold my hand, I hope." He glanced quickly in her direction.

And she felt a blush rise to her cheeks. "All the way across. And if I fall, I take you with me."

"Hmm. Guess I could think of worse people to take a swim with."

"Dr. Coborn, are you flirting with me?"

His brows flitted up. "Am I?"

"Me-thinks you are."

And she loved it. Definitely different from all their prior dates. Yes, she loved concerts and theater and dressing to the nines with a doctor at her side, but this casual, relaxed atmosphere was far more enjoyable.

"Now it's your turn, doctor." She turned in her seat as much as she could to face him before asking the next question, praying she knew his answer. "What is your plan to get Mom out of the apartment?"

Move back home whispered through her thoughts and became her hope.

"I've asked your father to move in with me."

She blinked, digesting his words. "Dad?"

"And then your mom can move back home."

"But..." That wasn't at all what Ronnie wanted. "Isn't he fine at home?"

"Not really." He turned on the blinker and passed someone going even slower than them. "We've been meeting together, and he's leery of being alone right now as he's been depressed. Moving in with me should help his mental attitude, and then your mom gets her home."

"But I thought..."

"What?"

"Oh, never mind." She felt a pout coming on, but couldn't stop it. Years of being a spoiled only child had taught her the pout worked well. But that was her parents, this was Gavin, who obviously didn't have a clue.

"Ronnie, don't shut me out. You have something to say, say it. I'm a big boy. I can take it."

She looked out the window at trees rushing past, suddenly wanting out of the car, and dreading the long day ahead. "It's just that I was hoping I'd be the one you'd be asking to move back home."

"Oh..."

Oh was right. She flicked her nails, but really wanted to kick something.

"I don't think we're ready."

"What if I do?"

He sighed and remained silent through several flicks of her nails. "Let's just take it a day at a time. Today's a good start."

Hmph. She hadn't intended to do that out loud. She really was a spoiled brat. And he was right to want to take things slow.

"Fine." She'd try a bit of humor to get things back on track. Hopefully, he'd catch on to the joke. "But if you fall in the Mississippi, it might just be because you were pushed."

"Oh really?"

"Yes, really." She looked at him to make sure he wasn't taking her seriously and breathed easier at the sight of his grin. "Hope you brought a change of clothes."

"That sounds like a threat."

"It just might be." She dared lay a hand on his arm that rested on his lap, and he didn't shake it off.

By the end of the day, she would be several steps closer to moving back in with her husband.

Chapter Twelve

Ronnie sat on the side of the river and took off her boots and socks while watching people, from toddler to grandfather, balance and wobble their way over slippery stones to walk across the Mississippi. It was hard to believe that the river that roared from the top of the United States down to the Gulf of Mexico began with a mere trickle over rocks spattered across a twenty- to thirty-foot-wide mouth. Such humble beginnings for a mighty river.

Maybe *humbly* was how the best things began. Just look at Jesus, born in a cave and placed in an animal trough. Evie had it so much better, but was she better for it?

She shivered and shook off the thought. Today wasn't a day for melancholy. She set her shoes aside and stood.

"Ready?" She offered a hand to Gavin and helped him stand.

"As I'll ever be."

"Aww, you'll succeed like you do with everything else."

"Except for sports."

That was something she didn't know about him. "Not an

athlete, huh?"

He shook his head. "And bullies love the uncoordinated, which made me try all the harder in academics."

Another thing she didn't know. Back when she was young, she probably was one of the bullies mocking the uncoordinated. "I'm sorry you went through that."

"Guess it made me stronger."

But bullying hadn't been necessary for his growth. "That makes me want to really teach Evie to be kind. I don't want her to grow up arrogant like her mom and grandparents."

"You're doing fine, Veronica."

"I can do better." She took his hand when their turn came to cross the river. "The rocks are super slippery, so be careful." She stepped on a stone and quickly withdrew her hand from his so she could balance.

She held her breath as her front foot sought purchase on a rock ahead. It slipped, and Gavin's hands immediately went to her waist.

"Who needs to be careful?"

"Ha ha ha." Finally, she gripped a stone in front and dared to reach for the next one. And the next. And another until she was three-quarters of the way across. She chanced a look in back of her and Gavin was several feet behind, his face a mask of concentration.

For a second, she considered razzing him, but then his comment about being picked on came back to her. From here on, she'd choose to be the encourager, not the bully.

"You're doing great," she said, taking her eye off her goal. Her foot slipped, and she screeched, but she quickly grasped onto a less slimy stone.

"You okay?" Gavin called from behind.

"I'm good." If she didn't want to make a drenching mistake, she was looking forward, not back.

With her foot, she examined the rocks ahead, searching for the sturdiest, least slippery one. Taking her time rather than rushing. Once she found the right stone, she moved forward. Usually the best foothold didn't lead her in a straight path, but as long as she made progress, that was what mattered.

With painstaking concentration, she reached for the next stone and the next until her foot melded with the sand on the other side.

"Yes!" She planted both feet on solid ground and did a little dance before turning back to watch Gavin. She thought her crossing had been meticulous. She could practically see the cogs turning in his brilliant mind, analyzing the pros and cons of each rock in his path before taking the next step.

Behind him, though, the crossers wore impatience in their rolled eyes and clenched fists.

"Come on, dude, just pick a rock and go."

Gavin's entire body tensed. Not a good omen for him making it across without taking a bath. As much as she wanted to put the bully in his place, she refrained. Instead, she concentrated on encouraging Gavin.

"Just three more steps and you're here."

He briefly looked up, smiled, then refocused on his task. Right foot. Left. Left again. Another right.

Then finally onto the sand.

Yes! She pumped her fists and high-fived her husband.

"Remind me not to do that again." He wiped his brow.

"Yow!" Behind them, the bully splashed face first into the river.

She and Gavin couldn't help but laugh along with the other crossers. The dude got what he deserved.

"Want to take the bridge back across?" She pointed up ahead. "Or walk through the river?"

He looked down at his jeans that he probably didn't want to get wet, so that made up her mind.

She sat beachside and rolled her pants up to her knees. "I'm going through. You're welcome to take the easy way."

"Sometimes easy is the best."

"True, but how often will you get a chance to say you walked through the Mississippi?"

"Is that a challenge?"

She shrugged. "Don't you like challenges?"

"Not unless it has to do with science."

"Hmm." She tapped her chin. "Then how do we make river crossing on foot a science project?" She snapped her fingers with an easy idea, at least for him. "Determine how far across the river is from this point." She drew an X in the sand right at the bank of the river. "To the pointy stone on the bank over there by walking across the river, heel-toe, heel-toe, taking in the depth of the river, judged by how far it comes up on your leg, and the length of your foot."

That brought out a grin and the steely grey in his eyes as he rolled up his pant legs to his knees. "Hopefully, that's high enough."

"If your pants get a little wet, it's not the end of the world."

He wrinkled his nose. "I genuinely dislike the feel of wet jeans."

"Your choice. I'm walking." She headed out into the river, turned and walked backward, appreciating the intensity on Gavin's face as he stepped forward into the river, no doubt careful to precisely land each foot while mentally cataloguing the river's depth. She should record this for Evie to see one day.

Ronnie took out her phone and turned on the video. She backed up slowly, carefully as he came toward her.

"Watch out!"

Her phone recorded a splash followed by Gavin being dunked sideways into the river by a black dog the size of a bear.

"Oh no." She hurried to him and offered a hand to help him up. Water dripped from his hair and beard and drenched his shirt and jeans. "I am so sorry."

He waved his arms, expelling water, then wrung his shirt while saying nothing. Only time would dry him out. He was probably torqued at her now. Why had she pushed?

"I really am sorry." She took his hand to lead him across.

But he tugged his hand away.

Oh he was upset. Made her want to hurl a curse word, but that would make him angrier yet.

"I need to finish."

Say what? "Finish?"

"Measuring." He walked back to the bank, to the X she'd drawn in the sand.

"Really, you're good."

He looked at her, that same grey steel grit in his eyes. "If I don't cross, if I don't get the measurement, it'll bother me."

She raised her hands in surrender. "Then go for it."

How many other guys would have just given up? Would have walked across, all grumpy, then blamed her? But Gavin wasn't any other guy.

Once again, she turned on her phone video to record his calculated crossing.

As before, he took deliberate steps across the river. She could practically see the cogs in his brain spinning.

At last, he touched his toe to the target stone and stood there silently for a moment. Then he looked over at her. "Twenty-five feet, three inches."

Seriously? "You figured it out already?"

He shrugged. "Simple math."

"Depends on who you talk to. I would have had to record every step. Then take a tape measure to my leg and foot before sitting down for hours trying to figure it out, only to throw my pencil at the wall, and I like math. How do you do that?"

He shrugged again. "Comes naturally." Then a sly grin filled his face, one she rarely saw. "Just like being a little sassy comes natural to you."

"Oh really." She narrowed the distance between them and poked his chest with her finger. "You think I'm sassy?"

"You think you're not?" His grin grew.

"That's not the point, mister." She balanced on her tippy toes to go face-to-soggy-face with him, and he didn't back away. She was on her way to a victory.

"I happen to like sassy." His nose came within a hair's width of hers.

Oh my. She could probably dry him off with the heat her body was emitting. It took every muscle in her being not to kiss him.

"Well, are you going to—"

"Excuse me. I'm sorry. So, so sorry." A woman hustled toward them, the leash in her hand leading the massive dog that had drenched Gavin.

Who stepped back.

Grrr. The woman better be sorry.

"The kids told me Grizzly knocked you down. He's just a puppy yet, and we're working on training him."

A puppy? How big was he going to get?

"But that's no excuse. And I'm sorry. Our campsite is within walking distance. I can't offer you a dryer, but we can light a fire for you."

"That's a generous offer." Gavin looked down at Ronnie. "What do you think?"

"I think you'd love it, and I would too."

"We'll gratefully accept your apology and your offer."

"Wonderful." The woman tugged on the leash. "Come on, Grizzly. Time to get you back home."

"We'll be right behind you." Ronnie sat in the grass to put her boots back on.

Gavin stood to put his on. He was getting bold after his journey across the river. Then he helped her stand and they jogged to catch up to the woman.

"We didn't catch your name." Gavin walked alongside the petite redhead. "I'm Gavin and this is..." He looked briefly at Ronnie. "This is my wife, Veronica. We're newlyweds."

Ronnie practically floated at his words. That had to mean she was welcome back home.

"You can call me Ronnie."

The woman turned down a dirt path that meandered through the woods. "I'm Amy, you met Grizzly, and my family's up ahead. They're a bit unruly, just to warn you."

"Sounds like fun." Ronnie gripped Gavin's hand, and he didn't pull away, but she heard him mumble something about it not sounding like fun. Chaos wasn't really his thing. They'd make their stay short and sweet, just long enough for him to get somewhat dry.

The tree canvas pulled back, revealing a campground filled with tents and RVs and a lot of kids playing.

Gavin gripped her hand tighter.

She whispered, "We'll make this quick."

"Thanks." A swift hand squeeze, then he let go. She heard him take a deep breath in preparation for donning his I-really-am-friendly costume.

Naturally, the greatest amount of chaos was centered at Amy's camp, both kids and adults playing cornhole, roasting marshmallows, having I-can-talk-louder-than-you conversations.

The exact situation Ronnie thrived in.

That Gavin hated.

After the river drenching and this, Gavin would want his home all to himself for weeks in order to recharge his introvert batteries.

Amy whistled, and the campers all looked to her and instantly quieted. She was definitely the leader of this unruly bunch. "Hey everyone, this is the couple that Grizzly dunked. I invited them here to dry off, so please use your best manners."

"Sorry 'bout that." A hulk of a man sauntered toward them, his voice as low as he was tall. He offered his hand. "Geoffrey."

"Gavin, and this is my wife, Ronnie."

Oh, she liked the sound of that.

"Nice to meet you both. Come have a sit at the fire. Can I get you somethin'? Coffee or cocoa?"

"Coffee would be marvelous." She looked up at Gavin for confirmation, and he nodded. "Thank you."

"Comin' right up." The man turned to the campfire. "Kids, get outta those chairs. Give 'em to company."

The kids scrambled up quickly and made themselves cozy on the ground.

"They obey without talking back?" From what she'd seen when she volunteered at church, backtalk was commonplace nowadays.

"Yep," said the large man who had fewer words than Gavin. "Not allowed."

Hopefully, Evie would be that easy to raise.

She and Gavin moved their camp chairs close to the fire, then Gavin stood, rotating himself around like a rotisserie chicken, to get dried off.

A minute later, the four adults were seated, each had a cup of hot coffee in hand, along with a roasting stick capped with a marshmallow.

"So what brings ya to Itasca?" Geoffrey pulled a flaming marshmallow back from the fire.

Gavin stretched an arm around Ronnie. "She thought it would make a good date. Guess she was right."

She looked wide eyed at him, and he winked. Oh, she was so confused. One minute, he was tense as congregants listening to a too-long sermon, the next he was flirting. Their car ride home would be interesting.

"So, Amy says you're newlyweds. On your honeymoon?"

"Just a getaway." Gavin answered for them. "The honeymoon is yet to be decided."

Did that mean they were debating whether to have a honeymoon or not?

"What about you?" Tired of the confusion, Ronnie turned the conversation from them. "Family vacation?"

"Yep." He gestured to the kids. "Some of these are ours. Some are cousins. Sort of an all-family break."

"Roarke, get down." Amy yelled at the smallest of children, who was attempting to climb up the side of the RV. He obeyed. For a moment, then began the climb again. "That child's giving us fits." Amy stomped over to the boy and pulled him down, then the two of them entered the RV.

She came out alone, but with aluminum-covered trays in

both hands, a bag of chips under each arm. "Lunch," she called out, and the children stampeded toward the table set up outside. "Hey, back off. Company first." She waved Ronnie and Gavin toward the spread of food on the table. "Come on up, get some before the kids eat it all gone."

Gavin stood. "We appreciate the hospitality, but we don't mean to barge in on your family time."

"Pshaw." Amy waved toward the ground. "Guests are always welcome."

Ronnie took Gavin's arm. "I think we should accept their offer, then we go home."

"No rush."

"Are you sure?" She whispered as they walked to the table. "I know stranger gatherings aren't your favorite."

"True. But this feels different. This feels like family."

She couldn't argue with him.

This couple and their kids felt real, like they didn't need to pretend they were someone "important" to be liked. They just were, and that was something she'd never experienced.

"If you're comfortable." She gave his hand a squeeze. "I am too."

With that, Gavin gave her a side hug and topped it with a kiss to her forehead. She couldn't recall him being so carefree.

A few hours, a bunch of food, and a few miserable cornhole games later, Gavin and Ronnie finally excused themselves to go home.

But where was "home" going to be for her?

She got in his cushy car and buckled in. Once they were

on the road, she'd bring up their living situation. She was ready to make the commitment, and by his actions today, Gavin was ready too. In their two years of dating, they hadn't had a day like today where they both loosened up and could be themselves.

She smiled and closed her eyes, ruminating over the day. The drive. The dunking. Meeting Amy and Geoffrey, who were now forever friends. Gavin even called her Ronnie, though she did like Veronica when used as an endearment.

"Veronica."

She opened her eyes and blinked. What happened to the sun?

"You're home."

What? She rubbed her eyes and stared hard out the windows. The moon and stars blanketed the sky that only moments before had been blue and sunlit. The door to her apartment building—

Apartment building? But she thought...

"We're not going back to your—our home?"

"Veronica..." He sighed. "We still have a lot to work out—"

"Yes. As husband and wife. I remember clearly that you introduced me as your wife."

"Because it's the truth."

"Not if you're not willing to live that way."

"I want that more than anything."

"Could have fooled me." She squeezed her door handle, and it didn't budge. He'd locked her in, the jerk.

"Veronica—"

"Just call me Ronnie like everyone else if you're going to

treat me like everyone else."

He sighed loudly. "You're much more than that."

"I don't understand." She sniffled but forbade any tears.

"Today was wonderful."

"*Was* is the definitive word."

"But it was one day. That's not enough to build a marriage on."

"Well, living apart certainly won't help either." She tried the door again. Still locked. "Let me out."

"Can you listen—"

"Now."

The lock clicked and she flung open the door, holding back from flinging a handful of words at him she knew she'd regret later.

"Ronnie."

She looked on the other side of the car where Gavin now stood.

"This. What's happening right now. This is why we're not ready yet. Do you understand?"

Not at all.

Without a goodbye, she stomped toward her apartment entry.

"Wait up. Let me walk you—"

She spun around and held up her hand like a stop sign. "As a single lady, I'm very capable of walking myself."

He only nodded. "The fact remains, we are married, and I still love you. But we have work to do."

Hah! She yanked her ring from her finger and tossed it at him. "That's what I think of your work."

Painful silence followed her into her home, the one she wouldn't be moving out of for a very long time.

Chapter Thirteen

onnie poured herself a coffee before preparing Evie's breakfast. She needed this quick pick-me-up after yesterday. Oh, she was a drama queen! It would serve her right if Gavin never wanted to see her again. She may not agree with his reasoning for not getting back together yet, but that didn't mean she should act the same age as her daughter.

"Hungry, Mama."

Actually, Evie probably acted older than she did.

"Coming, baby girl." Ronnie cut up strawberries and bananas and put them in their own partition in a sectioned plate. She added a quartered hard-boiled egg and a handful of Cheerios. Then she poured a pre-made smoothie into a toddler cup and brought it all to the dining table where Evie sat on a toddler seat.

She'd have to give Gavin a call later, when he'd be home from church, and apologize and find out exactly what he meant by having work to do.

She made herself a smoothie and a plate filled with the same foods as Evie's. She'd learned that Evie ate much better when Ronnie had the same food. She sat beside her daughter and forked a piece of egg.

"Pway." Evie clapped her hands together.

Surprised, Ronnie turned to her. One would think that being the daughter of a pastor, she'd have taught her own daughter to pray. Evie must have learned from Gavin, or even Kyle. At least the dads in her daughter's life were setting a good example, if not her grandparents and her own mom.

That would change right now. She closed her eyes and folded her hands, but words did not come. She could take the easy way out and ask Evie to pray, or she could recite the rote prayer they'd said when she was young. But if setting the example with nutrition was important, doing the same with Evie's spiritual life was even more crucial.

Gavin would advise her to keep it simple. Just speak the truth.

Her mouth went dry as she spoke. "Dear God, thank You for this day and for the food You've provided. In Jesus' name. Amen."

Oh, she sounded like a preschooler.

"That's one of the most genuine prayers I've heard from our family."

Ronnie jerked her head toward her mom, who entered the room dressed in her new khakis and blouse, her purse draped over her shoulder. Ronnie didn't want to dwell on her juvenile prayer, so she quickly changed the subject. "Going somewhere?"

"Well, church, naturally."

"Really?" Ronnie had thought her mom wouldn't ever set foot into True North again. "You don't care how people will react?"

"Dear, I'm not going back to that shrine your father built. I'm going to check out Emmanuel."

"As in, True North's competitor? Dad always said they were rigid."

Mom just looked at her, her lips scrunched, then shook her head. "Maybe some rigidity was what True North needed." She checked her watch. "If you hurry, there's still time for you and Evie to join me."

"I don't think I'm ready to go back yet."

"Suit yourself, but don't forget to think about my granddaughter."

There she went again, telling Ronnie how to parent, but Ronnie refrained from retorting. "Hope you enjoy it," she said with a smile, but couldn't contain her sarcasm.

"I know when I'm being dismissed. Your father certainly did it enough." Mom strode from the apartment, and the door closed quietly behind her, but it may as well have been a slam for the impact it had.

Was that how Dad had treated Mom? Ronnie hadn't noticed, but then she'd been the center of her father's world and could do no wrong. She'd observed nothing outside of her Dad-created bubble.

The doorbell rang, and Evie fought to be released from her booster seat.

"Stay put, baby girl." She hurried to the door. Had Mom left behind her keys?

She flung it open, and there stood the concierge with a bouquet of blue irises. Oh, they were beautiful!

"Thank you." She accepted the bouquet. "Wait one moment." She hurried to her cash jar in the kitchen, where she tossed bills and change that she didn't want stuffing her wallet, and grabbed a ten.

The man smiled broadly, accepting the tip. "If there's anything I can ever do for you."

"I'll let you know." She smiled at him as she was closing the door, then showed the irises to Evie. "Look what Dada Gavin sent us."

"Dada Gabin." She reached for the flowers.

"No touch. They need a vase. You keep eating." She carried the bouquet to the kitchen and set aside the attached card, though she wanted nothing more to rip open the envelope and read what Gavin had penned. After spending the day with him yesterday, she hadn't anticipated a delivery today. That made this all the more exciting.

In the kitchen, she dug out a crystal vase from her buffet, filled it with water, snipped the ends off the flowers, and then arranged them in the vase.

Beautiful. They would dress up her dining room table very nicely.

"There." She set the arrangement in the center of the table. "What do you think, Evelyn Joy?"

"Yay fwowers!" She clapped her egg-filled hands together, making a mess. Not that Ronnie cared at the moment.

"That's exactly what I say, baby girl. Yay flowers!" She slit the envelope with a knife and pulled out the card, a homemade one, of all things. And she laughed. The front was a picture from yesterday, of Gavin drenched. Apart from the letter inside, he had written, "Worth it, spending time with you. Love, Gavin."

Yeah, it had been worth it. If he hadn't gotten dunked by the dog, they never would have met the family, never would have enjoyed the picnic. She wouldn't have seen the casual side of Dr. Gavin Coborn.

"Look, Evie." She showed her daughter the card. "Dada Gavin got wet."

"I see." Evie reached for the card. For a second, Ronnie hesitated. She didn't want the card ruined. After all, how often was she going to get a homemade card from him, but with the added touch of Evie's fingerprints, it would be a true keepsake.

"Here you go." She handed the card to Evie, who hugged it against her cheek. "Wuv Dada Gabin."

"Me too, baby girl. Me too."

She opened the letter and sat back in her chair.

> *Dearest Veronica,*
>
> *I don't have a story for you today. Yesterday was <u>our</u> story. Thank you for pushing me beyond my comfort zone, for challenging me and encouraging me. Normally I'm uneasy with being stretched relationally, but with you it seemed effortless. That is one reason I love*

you so deeply.

But with that love comes my confession and contrition for being so poor at reading you last night. In bringing you to your apartment yesterday, I failed to take your feelings into consideration. It never occurred to me that for you the successful day meant you would be returning to our home. Not discussing it with you first was a grievous error on my part, for which I am deeply sorry. Believe me, I do not wish to hurt you.

We had an amazing day yesterday, the most memorable I've had with you. I saw a side of you I haven't experienced before, and I'm certain you'll say the same for me.

Just you and me.

Therein lies the problem. Our marriage cannot be just us, not if we want us to last.

Yesterday was a beautiful beginning, and I'm eager to continue. Our weekly Bible study is having an impact, and I delight in seeing curiosity for God in you. I anticipate the day when your curiosity blossoms into faith.

Until we speak again, know that I love you dearly,

Gavin

Confused, Ronnie laid the letter on her lap. Naturally, having grown up in the church, she knew what Gavin referred to—the verse about a cord made of three strands, instead of two, not being easily broken. The thing was, she did believe. She'd gone to church her entire life; how could she not believe?

Just because she wasn't fanatical about her faith didn't mean she didn't believe, did it?

Well, she'd show him.

"Evie, finish eating. You and Mama are going to church." Not True North, though. She wouldn't be caught dead setting one foot in that church again. Perhaps Mom had the right idea in checking out Emmanuel. It was large, like True North, so she could just go, blend in, and leave.

She checked service times. Obviously, she wouldn't make the service her mom was attending, and that was okay. But there was another service in an hour.

Once Evie finished eating, Ronnie cleaned her up and they headed out the door, Bible in hand.

Gavin would certainly be impressed and, for the logical thinker that he was, church attendance would be one more checkmark on his "Is Ronnie ready for marriage?" list.

Needing a shield from strangers who might want to ask too many questions of her, Ronnie kept Evie with her in the service. Dad would have frowned upon that—he hated being interrupted by children—but what her father liked no longer mattered.

She found an open chair near the back of the sanctuary, which was reminiscent of True North with its grand size. She sat next to an aisle so she could make a quick escape in case Evie became unruly. At least, that would be her excuse for leaving early.

Minutes later, the worship band filled the stage, people stood, and music exploded from the loudspeakers, yet not too loud to cover the congregants singing. Spotlights flashed across the room and over the stage, too much like True North.

After singing three songs, two of which Ronnie knew, they sat, and a hipster-looking man walked to the microphone, a Bible in hand. Along with a short-sleeved flannel shirt and cuffed jeans, he wore a full beard that had been popular in the 1800s. The dude was definitely trying too hard. At least Dad had never done that.

Kyle had though.

"I heard some of you snickering." The preacher's voice came over the speakers. "You took one look at me, and said, 'He's gone off the deep end.' You might not be wrong."

People chuckled.

"The thing is, this getup isn't me. You probably think I must be confused." He paused and surveyed the congregation. "It's easy to become confused in a world that claims everyone has their own truth, though. Some say, Jesus is my truth, others say Buddha is theirs, and others claim their truth is no god—small g—at all. In what might be my shortest sermon ever, I'm here to set the record straight."

Ronnie shifted in her seat. Some of her best friends didn't believe in God. Even her dad seemed ambivalent toward those who held other beliefs, saying they should pursue what was right for them. A loving God wouldn't condemn His children.

"Just one verse is all you need to set the record straight, so that's what I'm going to give you. Know that there are many, many more where this came from."

A verse popped up on a large screen in back of the pastor.

"I am the way, and the truth, and the life.
No one comes to the Father except through me."

One of the "I Am" statements they were going to be studying. She opened the Notes app on her phone. It was the sixth statement. After this sermon, she'd be steps ahead of the others, so she kept her app open to take notes.

"There's one word that's repeated three times in the first sentence. A word we often don't notice, but it might just be the most important word."

The? How could that be important?

The pastor continued as if he'd heard her thoughts. "Substitute the word, 'A' where 'The' is."

The revision flashed up on the screen, but it also flashed in her brain. *A way. A truth. A life.* That did make all the difference.

Then she reread the second sentence. *No one comes to the Father except through me.* Not a single person. She started breathing hard and gripped Evie against her chest so tight her daughter yelped. Sure, Ronnie had heard the verse before, often, but hadn't digested it.

Jesus was the only way. Wasn't there some other verse about entering through a narrow gate? Dad would know, of course. He was the one who'd taught her.

She heard little else of the sermon and snuck out the back door the second he said "Amen." As soon as she exited the building, she dialed Gavin. Dad may have taught her the words to the verse, but Gavin would show her the heart behind those words.

Chapter Fourteen

The phone rang five times before Gavin's voice mail picked up. Ronnie glanced at the time. Twelve thirty. Could he still be at church? Maybe. Suddenly desperate to understand that verse better, she needed to see Gavin ASAP. She'd try him again once she was in the car. She needed to see him.

Holding Evie, she hurried to her vehicle. Having left the service early, she would beat the rush of people leaving if she got on the road immediately.

She opened the back door and set Evie in her seat.

"No wike." She squirmed out of the seat.

"Doesn't matter, Evelyn." Ronnie buckled the fighting child into her seat. "It's to keep you safe."

Then the waterworks began.

Oh, this child was starting to have a diva attitude.

Wonder where she learned that from. Ronnie rolled her eyes at the thought. Like mother, like daughter. Just as Ronnie had learned her behaviors from her father. This cycle had to stop with her.

Letting Evie cry rather than coddling her as Ronnie

normally would, she got into the front seat of her Prius. She started the car and rolled toward the church exit already lined with cars. Guess she wasn't the only one thinking they could beat the rush.

Still, she was on the road within a minute. But where should she go? Home? Nah. The last thing she wanted was to spend time with her mother on Evie's final afternoon there. Tonight, she'd be shuffled to Kyle's for two weeks. Then two weeks back with Ronnie. Two weeks up here. Two weeks down there. It was enough to confuse anyone, let alone a child.

Where she went for the day depended on Gavin, so she tried calling again. Still no answer. Always wanting to be prepared in case his office tried to reach him, he usually kept his phone near him. Well, guess she'd just have to show up at his—or was it his *and her* house? She did have a key, so she could let herself in. They'd already prepared a nursery for Evie, so she could nap there.

Decision made.

Ronnie made a U-turn at the next intersection and aimed toward Gavin's home in an exclusive area north of Minneapolis. When she'd first seen the house, she'd fallen in love with it and had determined that she and Gavin would marry someday.

Their relationship had never been about love.

Not until he wouldn't let her back in.

Oh, she was a piece of work.

"Thanks, Dad," she said over Evie's whimpers.

But what about that commandment that said honor your

father and mother? What did that look like when your dad wasn't a good person? Another question for Gavin. Not that he had all the answers.

About twenty minutes of listening to Evie's cries later, she turned onto the long, winding drive leading to Gavin's home. Yes, Gavin's. She would not lay claim to it until they were officially back together.

She rounded the last corner and braked. Gavin's car was there, but so was her fathers. And a moving van.

Yes, Gavin had mentioned her father moving in with him, but she hadn't imagined it would become a reality. Especially this soon. What did that say for everyone getting back together?

Don't jump to conclusions, Ronnie.

She pulled up beside Gavin's car as he and her father came down the steps on the side of the garage. Gavin had a one-bedroom apartment up there, one he'd lived in until his parents had moved to Arizona, leaving the mansion to him.

So now her dad was going to live there?

She got out of her car, glanced in the backseat to see Evie sound asleep. Figured. Moving her would wake her, and then she wouldn't go down for an afternoon nap, and she'd be crabby the rest of the day, but leaving her in the car on this hot and humid July morning wasn't an option either.

Whether she woke Evie up now or drove home depended on Gavin's responses to her questions.

"Veronica." His face lit up when he saw her. That was a good omen, right?

"Hey." She nodded to her dad but didn't speak to him. Instead, she asked Gavin, "Do you have a moment?"

"For you? Always." Gavin met her halfway between her car and the home.

To her dad she said, "Can you keep an eye on Evie? She fell asleep in the car."

"Of course. Anything for my grandgirl."

"Thanks." Ronnie tossed him her keys. "Stay here with the AC on. Go for a drive. Whatever suits you."

Then she took Gavin's hand and led him to his backyard, to a wood bench nestled in a perennial garden he paid someone else to keep up.

He kept her hand in his when they sat, his thumb gently rubbing the backside. "I suppose you're surprised to see your father here."

Surprised? Maybe, but there was a different word for her feelings. "A little, but I guess I'm more disappointed. It tells me that you and I are a long way from getting back together. Not that I expected more, considering yesterday, and your letter today."

"I'm sorry, Veronica."

"No, I'm the one who's sorry."

"What do you have to be sorry for?"

She told him about the sermon this morning, at least the little she'd heard before walking out. About her surprise that she had never really understood that verse before. She loved how he listened without judgment.

"Isn't there a verse in the Bible about a narrow gate, too?"

"There is." He grew quiet, and she imagined his brain opening file drawers until it found what it wanted. "From Matthew seven, verses thirteen and fourteen. It says, 'Enter by the narrow gate. For the gate is wide and the way is easy that leads to destruction, and those who enter by it are many. For the gate is narrow and the way is hard that leads to life, and those who find it are few.'"

She shook her head, always amazed by his mind. "And I've been aiming toward the wide gate."

He remained silent, affirming her statement.

"And True North, AKA Dad, has pointed its members to the wide gate."

His thumb made circles on her hand, his gaze outward. "That's changing."

"For Dad or True North?"

"Both."

"You've still been attending?"

"I figured I could abandon a sinking ship or do what I could to help keep it afloat. I chose the latter."

"How's that going for you?" She looked directly at him, needing to see his expression.

He grinned. "Doing a lot of bailing, but the water level's going down." His smile faded. "Sometimes it takes a tragedy for people to see the truth."

"The truth." She looked toward the big house she'd loved. "Like me loving your degree, your job, your home."

His head bowed, and his thumb stilled, but he didn't release her.

"Like True North, that's changing." She squeezed his

hand and touched his cheek, hoping to get him to look her way. It worked. "Before we married, I had feelings for this." She spread her arms, indicating the house and property. "I was a spoiled, arrogant diva who tore apart my family and ensured that Evie would spend her life being shuffled from one parent to the other."

"Veronica—"

She held up her hand. "I've been aiming for that wide gate, thinking I can do whatever I want in life, but all that did was hurt the people I love, you being one of them."

Ashamed, she had to look away. He'd been so good to her, and she'd responded with selfishness.

His thumb continued to circle on her hand. "There's plenty of blame to go around. I shouldn't have pushed you. I should have waited until you were spiritually ready for the commitment."

"I'm not there yet." She shook her head.

"Still bailing?" There was a smile in his voice.

"Yeah, but making progress."

"I can tell."

She inhaled and let it out slowly. "I have some questions."

"I expected as much."

Her phone buzzed with a text message. She unconsciously reached for it, then stopped herself. Whoever it was could wait.

"Dad's moving in. For how long?"

Gavin shrugged. "As long as it takes."

"For what? For him and Mom to get back together?"

"If that happens."

If…

"So that means Mom will probably move home."

"Your father said that's their plan."

Hallelujah for that, anyway. "You'll still host our Bible study on Wednesday?"

"If you'd like me to."

"You have a lot of 'ifs.'" She longed for more predictability.

"Life is full of uncertainties."

Yes, yes, it was, and all her longings wouldn't change that. "I guess that leaves me with the most important question then."

His thumb stilled and his hand tensed. Likely, he was anticipating a different question, but she now realized that Gavin had been right about their marriage beginning on a rocky foundation. As usual, he remained quiet. Always the listener. One more thing she loved about him.

"Do you suppose the two of us could start over? Do the old-fashioned courtship thing?"

Silence.

Followed by him shifting on the bench.

"Sounds intriguing," he finally answered. "Would you like me to ask your father for permission?"

She laughed. "Absolutely."

Ronnie smiled all the way home, even with Evie whining in the back seat. The fragments of her life were being pieced back together. Maybe not the way she'd anticipated, but that was okay.

She glanced at Evie in her mirror. Unfortunately, some pieces would never fit together nicely. Going ahead, though, with her and Kyle getting on the same page spiritually, their daughter would have a chance to grow up a lot less broken than the two of them had been.

Naturally, Evie had fallen asleep by the time they arrived home. That meant Kyle was going to have his hands full tonight. But he could do it. He was a good father.

It sure felt good to admit that.

More truth.

She carried the limp child up to her apartment. Inside, her mom's luggage sat in the entry. Apparently, she wasn't wasting any time moving back home. Ronnie should be thrilled.

But this night might be her first alone since before her marriage.

"Is something the matter?" Mom always seemed to intuit Ronnie's feelings.

"You're leaving."

"Isn't that what you wanted?" Mom reached for Evie.

"Yes." She handed over the sleepy child. "Just feeling a little melancholy. Kyle's picking up Evie tonight. I'll be alone."

"Would you like me to stay?"

"Not necessary." Ronnie shook her head. "I'll make some

popcorn and put in a chick flick."

"I can at least stay for that." Mom shifted Evie to her other hip. "One last mother-daughter night?"

Sounded perfect, actually. "I'd like that. But for now, we need to awaken Sleeping Beauty here and feed her before Kyle arrives. How about some mac-e-cheese, baby girl?"

Evie's eyes popped open at the mention of her favorite food.

"Guess that's a yes."

So together, the three ate their pasta, then Ronnie packed Evie's little backpack. This had always been Evie's life, but Ronnie would never get used to it.

Her phone hummed, indicating she had a guest. Kyle. She buzzed him up and prepared for the hard goodbye. Not for Evie. She loved her Dada.

A minute later, her doorbell rang, and she waved Kyle into the apartment.

Surprise lit his face. They'd always done the exchange at the door with neither crossing the threshold.

"Dada!" Yep, there would be no tears from Evie.

"Hey, Cadenza. How's my big girl?" He scooped her up into his arms, and she squeezed his neck with a hug a python would be envious of.

"Wuv you."

"I love you, too." He looked to Ronnie. "She's ready to go?"

Ronnie nodded and handed him the backpack. He probably thought she was being rude, but if she spoke, her wobbly voice would convey her sorrow.

He aimed for the door, then turned back. "Um, I have something to tell you."

"Okay." She crossed her arms, wishing he would just leave so she could go cry in her room.

"Trip and I, we're getting married."

Ronnie stood there. Numb. Not knowing what emotion to feel. Yes, she was technically married, but this was Evie's father, the first man she'd loved, even if it had been a selfish love.

Finally, she shrugged. "I don't know what to say. Congratulations?"

"The wedding's two weeks from yesterday."

Two weeks? That meant one thing. "Why the rush? She pregnant?"

His face flushed and his eyes flashed. "No, she's not. We love each other, so why wait?"

"I'm sorry." Avoiding his gaze, she stroked Evie's back. "I wish you two the best."

"Appreciate it." He turned to go.

But she couldn't leave it at that. "One more thing."

He turned at the hip, with his feet still aiming for the door.

"I want you to know I'm sorry. For everything."

His eyes softened. "Yeah, me too. We did a good job of messing up our lives."

"And Evie's."

"Especially Evie's."

"But I'm working on cleaning up the mess."

He turned his full body toward her. "If there's anything I

can do…”

“Just be a good dada to Evie, okay?”

“That's a promise I can easily keep.”

Ronnie stood facing the door as Kyle left with their daughter. He hadn't belonged to her for nearly two years, since she'd kicked him out because she had Gavin. Still, with his upcoming marriage, the last little bit of hold she had on him was being ripped away, and as much as logic told her that was inevitable, tears still found their way to her eyes.

“I heard what he said.” Mom laid a hand on her shoulder. “I'm sorry, honey. He's a good man.”

Ronnie turned and hugged her mom like she had when she was little.

Mom stepped back. “I think this calls for a tear-inducing chick flick and lots of popcorn to commemorate the men being permanently severed from our lives.”

Wait. What? “Permanently?”

Mom's jaw grew rigid and she spun away. “I meet with an attorney tomorrow to begin the divorce proceedings.”

Chapter Fifteen

"How can she do this to Dad?" Ronnie paced the floor of Gavin's library with Gavin sitting silently, always listening. When she'd called him shortly after Mom delivered her blow, he'd insisted she come over to talk. This kind of conversation wasn't meant for the phone.

"Does she throw forty years away for one mistake?" A massive mistake that Ronnie found difficult to forgive, but still... Hadn't they vowed to love each other for better or for worse?

She turned to him, made sure his gaze connected with hers. "What are we going to do to keep them together?"

"Veronica." He patted the space beside him on the settee.

She complied, but hadn't finished venting. "And what does Dad say? Is he just going to lie down and accept it? Does he even know?"

"He knows." Gavin took her hand. "That's what prompted him to accept my invitation to move in to the guesthouse. Admittedly, he doesn't have much hope for their marriage at this moment."

"Then how do we give them hope?"

"It's not up to us."

She opened her mouth to object, but clamped it shut. Shook her head. "I feel so helpless."

"We're not." He folded his hands around hers. "We can be vigilant in prayer."

"Do you really believe that will work?"

He sat quietly, looking upward for a moment, then at her. "The results we desire aren't promised us, but God will hear our prayers, and He will give us peace regardless of the outcome."

"And that gives us hope."

"Yes, it does."

"Can we pray now?"

"Now is always the best time." He bowed his head. Was silent. Waiting for her? What if she flubbed up? Sounded more childish than Evie?

None of that mattered, not when her parents' marriage was on the line, so she cleared her throat and found the words. "Lord, You know I'm not good at this praying thing. Hard to believe since I grew up in the church, but I'm working on it. Anyway, thanks for loving me even though I've ignored You. Thank You for the love of this man beside me, though I really am not worthy of him. And thank You for my beautiful baby girl that neither Kyle nor I deserve. Guess it took this mess for me to realize how much You really do care for us."

Gavin squeezed her hands with the gentlest of touches. For a man who was normally socially awkward, he was sure mastering how to show love.

And that gave her courage to continue. "We do have one more request. I hate to see what this is doing to Mom and Dad. Yes, Dad messed up in a way that still confounds me, but I've learned that You love him anyway. Can You restore the love between them? Help Mom forgive? Help them see You again?"

Gavin's thumb caressed the back of her hand. So gently, goosebumps spread across her body.

"And Lord, thank You for this beautiful woman praying with me. Thank You for opening her eyes to see You, and I pray that each day she'll grow in her love and knowledge of You as You've helped me grow. In Your holy name, amen."

A reverent hush swaddled them, and they sat together with hands folded and heads bowed, listening for several minutes.

Then Gavin squeezed her hands and released them. Brushed his lips across her forehead. "Thank you," he whispered.

All she could do was nod, overcome by the warmth of his love.

"Would you mind if we made this a weekly event, praying for your parents?"

"I would like that. Along with our Wednesday devotion."

"Even if your mother or father choose not to come?"

"Absolutely. And let's not forget you're courting me." She inched closer to him.

He grinned. "How could I forget that?"

"The important question is, then, at what point is it okay

for me to kiss you?"

He cupped his hand on her cheek. "Now?"

Oh my, his gentle touch sent shivers throughout her body. "Now is always the best time."

She feathered her lips over Gavin's then rested her forehead against his. "That's probably good for now, because Dr. Gavin Coborn, I am falling heels over head in love with you."

Chapter Sixteen

Late November

Giddy with anticipation, Ronnie scrunched curls into her hair, preparing for her evening with Gavin. Was tonight the night they'd resume their lives as husband and wife? She was more than ready. Had been for months.

Had it already been over four months since Mom had moved out? Five since Dad had been arrested? More importantly, five since she and Gavin started to learn what love really was. They'd spent every week praying together, studying the Bible together. After completing the "I Am" statements, they'd moved on to the names of Christ.

He'd also continued the Sunday notes and flowers. With each passing week, the notes became more intimate as he learned to reveal his heart.

The "Hallelujah Chorus" played in the background as she touched up her makeup. "Wonderful Counselor. Almighty God. Prince of Peace." Just three of Jesus' names. There were over fifty in the Bible!

She blew out a breath and stepped back to get the full view in the mirror. She looked pretty good, if she did say so herself. The sequined burgundy sheath hugged her curves just enough for Gavin to notice, yet not too tight, allowing her to move freely.

No doubt, Gavin would look just as nice.

Her doorbell rang as if hearing his name. Stiletto-heeled shoes in hand, she hurried to the door, flung it open, and had to catch her breath. Hard to believe she'd once thought Gavin to be a nerd. With no glasses and a closed-cropped beard, along with his slim fitting charcoal suit, he'd turn every female head in the restaurant.

She could proudly say that he belonged to her.

He let out a low whistle. "I'm speechless."

"Exactly the response I was aiming for." She reached up on her tippy toes to give him a kiss that let him know she was ready to be his wife in every way.

And he didn't complain or break the kiss early, which mean that he was on the same wavelength. She was packed already, just in case.

She ended the kiss and wiped his lips with a tissue. Ah, there was the blush she loved to see, though it was becoming rarer as they grew together.

"Ready to go?" He gestured to the shoes still draped from her fingers.

"Just need my coat, if you wouldn't mind."

He pulled her coat from the closet and helped her put it on, then she stepped into her shoes. She loved the way they made her legs look, but her feet still protested the pinch.

Twenty minutes later, they pulled up to the supper club that promised delectable food and an evening of dancing. Gavin swore he had two left feet, which was probably true, but if he just held her and swayed, that was all she'd need.

He let the valet take his sedan, then he escorted her into the room that was already decorated for Christmas. Her favorite holiday that was now less than a month away. She couldn't wait to put the finishing touches on Gavin's—her—home.

A band softly played Christmas tunes in the corner of the room as the maître d' led them to their table, a corner booth for privacy.

"Thank you." Gavin shook the man's hand, likely palming a nice tip for the perfect table.

"And thank you." Ronnie looked across the table at her husband. Yes, her husband, though she hadn't dared think of him that way during the past months. They'd had too much growing to do. Especially her. They still did, for that matter, but they could grow as husband and wife.

She picked up the menu that displayed no prices, and names of dishes she couldn't pronounce.

"What are you thinking of getting?" She'd take a cue from him.

"Probably the *côte de bœuf.*"

"Which is?"

"Sorry." He smiled apologetically. "Prime rib."

"Hmm. That sounds too heavy for me tonight." With her nerves on high alert waiting for him to invite her back home, she couldn't think of eating meat.

"You may enjoy *le salade Bagration*. It has lettuce, a thin pasta, chicken, artichoke heart, wedged tomatoes, celery, and mayonnaise."

"Perfect." She closed her menu, and a second later, a waiter appeared.

Gavin relayed their order then stood and offered, "Would you care to dance?"

"I would." She laid her hand in his and he helped her stand.

He led her onto the dance floor where he tucked his hand on the small of her back and gently pulled her close.

Ah, he smelled of mint. She rested her head on his shoulder and let him lead the slow dance. The song ended too soon.

"You've been practicing," she whispered as the next song began.

"I've been taking lessons," he spoke into her hair, sending shimmies down her spine.

"When have you had time for lessons?" In between work and all his Bible studies, he'd barely had time to sleep.

"Lunchtime. They came to work. My office enjoyed watching this klutz learn to dance."

"And no one snitched."

"Not if they wanted to keep their job." He laughed.

It was funny because Gavin wasn't the type to bribe his employees into silence.

She leaned against him, swaying along to his perfect rhythm. Oh, she could get used to this.

Too quickly that song ended, and he led her back to the table.

The waiter must have been watching because moments later, their food was delivered.

Gavin reached across the table for her hand and thanked God for the food. A mere six months ago, she would have been embarrassed by the overt display, now she didn't care what onlookers thought.

"And thank You for blessing me with this dear man," she added to Gavin's "Amen."

He squeezed her hand and let go.

She picked at her salad. It was tasty, but her stomach nerves had turned into jumping jellybeans.

"Don't you care for it?" Gavin asked while sawing a piece of his prime rib.

"I do." She shrugged. "Just not hungry I guess."

"Too bad." He forked a piece of her lettuce. "It's very good."

Yes, it was, but with the thought, the hope, that he was going to welcome her home tonight hovering over the table, she had no appetite. If he didn't bring it up before they left, she would. But in the meantime, to get her mind off things, she needed to make conversation.

She scooped a half size bite of salad and held it midair. "How is Dad doing?"

"Better every day. Believe it or not, he's loving his retail job. Gives him good contact with people. He's finding he's a better minister outside the church than he was in."

"Hard to believe." She chewed on her meal. "What about signing the divorce papers? Mom's getting impatient."

Gavin offered a sideways grin. "She's going to have to be

patient. Sounds like he isn't going to sign. Says he plans to fight for his marriage."

"And Mom gave up right away."

"At least your father is now at peace. What he did troubles him, probably always will, but he now knows the depth of God's forgiveness. That's what he'll be talking about next Sunday at True North."

She couldn't believe Dad was going back to True North. That they'd let him in the doors. "I'll do my best to get Mom there. Think I could coerce her if it meant not seeing Evie for a month?"

"That would certainly do it." He laughed.

"Well, we need to keep praying for her. She's become so bitter. Hearing Dad's talk could help."

"We'll redouble our efforts tomorrow. We're holding on to hope."

"It is that season."

"Your place, right? Can't wait to get my hug from Evelyn."

Her too. "Can't believe she's eighteen months old already."

"And talking more than a pastor."

She laughed. "That's for sure."

Okay. Enough small talk. She set down her fork and watched Gavin eat as if he had nothing else on his mind.

Maybe he didn't. Maybe she'd read his signals wrong.

"Problem?" He finally looked at her.

She shrugged. "Just not hungry."

"Well then." He put down his fork and knife and stood,

offered his hand. "Why don't we just dance instead?"

She rested her hand in his. "I'd like that."

They danced to "White Christmas," "The Christmas Song," and "All I Want for Christmas is You." She'd thought for certain that would be the moment he'd lean over and whisper in her ear, "I want you to come home." The band played "What are You Doing New Year's Eve?" followed by "I'll Be Home for Christmas" and "A Christmas Love Song."

Still nothing. And her feet were getting sore. Her eyes droopy.

"Tired?" He whispered a kiss across her forehead.

She nodded.

"One more song, and we'll go."

The band started playing "Silent Night," and Gavin pulled her closer. She could easily fall asleep in his arms.

"Veronica Joy," he said with beautiful tenderness. "You've filled my life with joy. Hope. You've helped me break out of my shell, if only a little bit. I didn't know what love was until these last months."

He pulled back.

And excitement awoke the butterflies that had gone dormant in her stomach. Tonight, they'd start again as husband and wife. Suddenly, she was no longer tired.

Then he was down on one knee. Opening a ring box.

She blinked, trying to comprehend what she was seeing. Why would he propose? They were already married.

He was speaking, but she missed his first words.

"...now that our love is strengthened by the third strand of cord, this coming Christmas Day, would you marry me again? Renew our vows?”

Renew their vows...

He'd stunned her silent. And then a handful of tears escaped. Of course he'd want to renew their vows. He loved her too much to do anything else.

“Veronica?”

She looked down at his face, pinched with worry and knelt down in front of him. She cradled his face in her hands. “I can't think of anything I'd rather do.”

Chapter Seventeen

Ronnie clung to Gavin's gloved hand as they walked over a shoveled sidewalk among a crowd of other latecomers toward True North Church. Had it really been six months since she'd set foot inside the building? It seemed like forever, but then it felt like just yesterday that her world had tipped upside down.

Mom strode ahead of them, her head high, clearly trying to ignore the stares, backward glances, and loud whispers. Ronnie tried to ignore it as well, but still felt the heat of the congregation's derision.

But Mom had changed since that day Dad messed up. She'd updated her look, but downgraded her empathy meter, at least from Ronnie's perspective. The only reason Mom attended today was because Dad had promised to sign the divorce papers if she came and listened to him.

And that broke Ronnie's heart. Still, she and Gavin continued to lift Mom in prayer.

She looked down at her hand, at the ring there, a promise to love, honor, and cherish through whatever trouble arose. Interesting how Dad's mess-up had actually brought her and Gavin closer together, and deepened her faith to a level she hadn't realized was possible. So for that she gave thanks.

Gavin hurried ahead to open the door for Mom, who acknowledged the action with a bow of her head before entering. He remained there until Ronnie caught up.

She inhaled a deep breath then stepped over the church's threshold. The air squeezed her, and seemed to steal her breath.

Gavin gripped her hand, leaned over, and whispered, "You're doing fine."

Yeah, well, she didn't feel so fine. She kept her head down as she and Gavin followed Mom to the coatracks, then into the sanctuary, to the back row. No surprise, Mom claimed the end seat for a quick getaway. Ronnie would likely be right behind her. If they could steal away from church after Dad's talk without speaking to anyone, she'd be ecstatic.

The countdown to service beginning flashed on one of the large screens at the front of the sanctuary. Ten...nine...

Her stomach raging like a winter blizzard, Ronnie looked down, closed her eyes, prayed for calm, for a listening ear. The last time she'd heard Dad speak—preach—here, he'd been the confidant man she'd grown up admiring. Now she realized her perception of confidence was actually arrogance. She couldn't imagine him having the same attitude today.

She startled as loud music broke into her prayer. People around her were standing, clapping, raising their hands. Some were singing, but she couldn't hear them above the music. That was one thing she'd appreciated about Kyle's church—she could actually hear those around her sing.

Still, she followed Gavin's lead and sang along, trying to focus on the words and not the show around her. She lost herself in the lyrics, singing of Jesus being the friend of sinners, followed by a song that spoke of Jesus being our living hope.

Truth.

She prayed those around her would also take in the lyrics, that they would experience their faith on a deeper level.

Too soon, the music ended, and the man who'd been one of the associate pastors stepped up to the microphone. Dad had once called him a troublemaker, but Gavin respected the man. In her eyes, that boded well for True North.

"When I came to True North." The pastor looked out at the congregation. "Fresh from seminary, wide-eyed and ready to spread the gospel, I had the privilege of being mentored by a dedicated servant of God. I watched in awe of what he was doing here and put him up on a pedestal. I think that's true of many in our church. The problem with placing a human above the rest is that they will fall. It's our nature. And he did fall. Hard. And those of us who placed him on that pedestal were also the first to stomp him further into the ground. Myself included."

Ronnie sat up straight, the pastor having hooked her attention.

"So, when Pastor Dean approached me a few weeks back asking if he could speak with all of you, I bucked at the idea.

Didn't want him influencing *my* church anymore."

He looked around the church with the dramatic pause preachers are so good at. "That's when God bonked me over the head. Literally. Moments after I spoke with Pastor Dean, a book—the Bible!—fell off my shelf, clipped the back of my head and I heard the words almost as clearly as you're hearing me today, 'Whose church?'"

The pastor looked down at the podium then back at the congregation. "I'm embarrassed by how easily I fell into the pride trap, and for the first time realized that Pastor Dean was just as human as I was. As you are. And Jesus loves and forgives him just as all of us want to be loved and forgiven. When Pastor Dean and I spoke last week, I realized for the first time the beauty that God can create from our messes. Please welcome back Pastor Dean Whitmer."

Some polite applause. A lot of snickers. Too much silence as Dad walked to the stand, looking smaller than he used to appear, yet more confident. He carried his Bible, the one he'd purchased new prior to their "I Am" Bible study, but now seemed worn as if he'd had it for years. He set the Bible on the podium, bowed his head for a few tense moments, then looked up.

Beside her, Mom sat straight, her chin up, cheeks taut, but her hands wrung in a nervous dance.

"Thank you, Pastor Hans, for your generous introduction. You are correct. God can take broken pots like myself and create a thing of beauty."

He looked out at the congregation, scanning the people. Searching for her and Mom maybe? She raised her hand even with her head and he seemed to connect with her. He smiled, nodded, looked back at the podium.

"Let me first say that I am deeply sorry for the pain I've caused all of you. For the division my actions knifed not only at True North but in the Christian community. A shepherd is supposed to keep their flock safe, not lead them off a cliff, which was exactly what I did. More so, I'm sorry for the rift my actions caused in my family, especially with my dear wife, Cheryl, a chasm so wide that no bridge can cross it. That is my doing, alone."

Mom just huffed. Would she never forgive him?

Ronnie wished she could run up onstage, give him a hug right now, encourage him, because she knew his heart was breaking over the demise of his marriage.

"I encourage you to use my example as how not to lead a church. In order to grow our congregational numbers, I became lax with God's word. Rather than teaching the truth, I taught what would make the outside world love us. Popularity became my god."

Dad paged through his Bible and held it up. "In Matthew and Luke, you'll find Jesus' parable teaching about the lost sheep. A true shepherd will leave his herd of ninety-nine and go find the lost one. What I did instead was encourage that lost one to explore, rather than bring them back to the fold. In the parable of the prodigal son, when the son asked for his inheritance, the father grieved his son's departure. I gave you my blessing to leave. I told all of you—including my own daughter—to follow your hearts, rather than to follow God. Jeremiah 17:9 tells us the heart is deceitful and desperately sick. I ignored that verse in my desperation to be loved, but the love I sought wasn't true love."

Mom's head was now bowed. Her hands stilled. What was she thinking? Was any of what Dad said getting through to her? Or did she believe this was just another flimflam act, with Dad trying to sucker people in?

"Real love is sacrificial, not selfish, and I was unbelievably selfish in my leadership. For that I'm deeply sorry and seek your forgiveness, though I know I don't deserve it. Matthew 10:39 tells us 'Whoever finds his life will lose it, and whoever loses his life for my sake will find it.' Folks, that is real love. In a few weeks, we'll be celebrating Christmas. God sent His only Son to earth. For us, a desperately broken people. That's real love. Jesus dying on the cross, taking our punishment, that's real love. It took my falling off my self-built pedestal to realize that."

Dad closed his Bible and once again looked out at the congregation. "Thank you for listening." Then he looked down at Pastor Hans seated in the front row. "Thank you for giving me a platform to share my story."

Pastor Hans nodded.

Dad took a breath, licked his lips, focused again on the congregation with none of the arrogance he used to display. "I'd like to leave you with a verse that has become instrumental in my life. 1 Timothy 1:15 says, 'The saying is trustworthy and deserving of full acceptance, that Christ Jesus came into the world to save sinners, of whom I am the foremost.'"

He bowed his head.

And she felt Mom get up. Watched as Mom hurried out the back doors of the church. She wouldn't get far since Gavin had driven her there. One more piece of insurance that Mom would attend.

For a second, Ronnie debated following her, to wrap Mom in a much-needed hug. But at this moment, supporting her father was her priority.

As Pastor Hans delivered the remainder of his sermon, Dad came around the side of the sanctuary and found them in the back row. His face drooped when his gaze landed on Mom's empty chair.

So, Ronnie stood and gave him a hug. She whispered, "I've never been prouder of you."

His shoulders straightened and he sat next to her through the remainder of the service, her hand encompassed in his, like it used to be when she'd been a child.

She had her daddy back. Praise God for that!

The pastor ended the service with a prayer, then Ronnie grabbed Gavin's hand, planning to pull him from the sanctuary before others left, but the couple in front of them turned around.

Her shoulders tensed as she waited for the vitriol directed toward Dad.

"Thank you, Pastor Dean." The woman offered her hand. "Know that you are forgiven."

The simple words brought tears to her eyes.

And Dad's.

But now they were trapped. More people stopped to speak with Dad. Offered their forgiveness. Sought his advice for cleaning up their own messes.

"I'm out of the counseling business." Dad expounded to many who stopped. "My best advice is to remain in prayer and the Word."

A half hour later, they finally escaped the back row.

Ronnie rushed to find Mom. She checked the women's lounge, the coffee shop, library, fellowship hall. No sight of her. She tried Mom's phone. No answer. Then returned to the entry where Dad and Gavin awaited with her winter coat.

"Nothing?" Gavin asked as he helped her into her coat.

"Not a sign." She checked her phone again. Tried calling. "Help me check all the rooms?"

Gavin nodded.

"And I'll stay here in case she shows up." Dad tugged on his gloves.

She and Gavin checked every room in the church. The bathrooms. Sunday school rooms. Even the janitor's closet. Her blood temperature rose with each empty room. They returned to the entry find Dad in conversation with Pastor Hans.

He looked up. "Nothing?"

"Nope. And I'm teed off that she'd take off and not even leave a message." Ronnie stuffed her phone in her purse then pulled her gloves from her pockets. "If for some reason she's still here, she can find her own way home."

"I'm guessing that's what already happened." Gavin put his arm around her, probably in an attempt to calm her. But after Dad's talk, how could her mom be so selfish?

"Then let's go find her." Ronnie strode toward the exit doors and didn't slow until she reached Gavin's car. He'd tripped the locks and the auto start, so she got into a warm car with luxuriously heated seats. They certainly wouldn't help her cool off.

Dad got in the back seat. "Don't bother bringing me home first. I want to check on Cheryl." Worry came through his voice.

Didn't know what he was worried about. Mom was an adult who could take care of herself. Ronnie just wanted to give her a good talking to.

Several minutes later, they drove up a snow-coated driveway to Mom's home. Tracks of a vehicle that had pulled in then backed out were apparent.

That made her blood boil even more. In the few short weeks Mom had lived with Ronnie, she'd insisted knowing all the details of Ronnie's comings and goings. The least she could do was return the favor.

They all got out of the car. Ronnie tried opening the front door. Locked. Dad took out his key, and it didn't work. That wasn't a surprise. Mom had probably changed the locks first thing after moving home.

Gavin ran through the snow to the basement door. Also locked.

Way to go, Mom.

Ronnie raised her hand to press the doorbell.

A loud crash penetrated the windows from inside the house, followed by bloodcurdling scream.

They had to get in there. Now.

Chapter Eighteen

"I'll break a window."

Ronnie nodded to Gavin, who hustled to his trunk and hurried back with a lug wrench.

"My dime," he said while swinging the wrench at the front window. It shattered into a zillion pieces. With the wrench, he brushed away the shards from the sill, then he took off his coat, laid it across the sill and climbed through. A second later, he opened the front door.

"I heard something back here." Gavin led the way down the short hall to the master bedroom, and stopped in the doorway. He stretched his arm across the hallway, preventing Ronnie from seeing what was in the room.

No, no, no. She had visions of her mom lying in a puddle of blood.

She ducked under his arm, and pushed him aside.

And froze.

Mom sat on the edge of the bed, her face cradled in her hands. Around her, every picture that had been on the wall, every knickknack from her dresser, all the clothes from her closet, lay strewn and broken on the floor.

"Jesus, give me words," Ronnie whispered.

But Dad pushed past her and sat beside Mom. "Cheryl." He stretched an arm around her back.

"Come." Gavin took Ronnie's arm and tried to lead her away.

She shook it off.

"Please," he said in a near whisper.

She skewered Gavin with a look, then turned to her parents huddled together on the bed. Okay, fine. Gavin was right as usual.

She felt like stomping down the hall like a scolded child, but behaved herself. Instead she went to the kitchen. Turned on the coffeemaker. Found brownies in the cookie jar and set a dozen on a plate. Then she sat beside Gavin on the living room couch and waited.

A good half hour and four brownies later—just for her—Mom and Dad came out of the bedroom.

His hand pressed to her back and her face mottled red and pink from sobbing. Her hand was wrapped with a stocking, but blood evidenced she wasn't okay. They sat together on the loveseat. Didn't even try to put distance between them.

Ronnie didn't know what to say, how to react, but managed to eek out, "Are you hurt?" Dumb question. Obviously, she was hurt.

"She should have it looked it," Dad said. "Might need stitches."

But Mom shook her head, keeping her injured hand in her lap.

Ronnie took the hint that Mom would speak when she was ready, but it wasn't easy to remain quiet.

Several minutes and two more brownies later, Mom said something, but she said it so softly, Ronnie couldn't make out her words.

"I'm sorry." Ronnie leaned closer to hear better. "I didn't underst—"

"Your dad wasn't the only one at fault." That came out clear and concise, and pinned Ronnie to the back of the couch.

Mom glanced between her and Gavin. "You think your father was alone on that pedestal?"

Ronnie gulped, not knowing what answer to give, if Mom even wanted one.

"I helped him climb right on up." Mom jabbed her chest with her finger. "I enjoyed the attention. I'm just as much to blame for leading the sheep astray as he was." She wiped her eyes. "But it wasn't until your father stood up there this morning that I realized I was as much at fault for his fall as him. I'm as much at fault for not guiding you and Kyle on the right path, for pushing you toward Gavin. It's only through a miracle of God that Gavin has turned out to be a far godlier person than both your father and me. That you, dear Veronica, have grown a faith I'm now envious of."

Ronnie still didn't know what to say, but she knew exactly what to do. She left Gavin's side and squished between her parents, like she used to when she was little. She hugged them both.

"Guess we were quite the trio at True North," she said,

trying to inject a little humor.

Dad chuckled. Mom did not.

"Which is why I've agreed to go to counseling with your father." Mom reached across Ronnie's lap, and Dad took her hand. "We've got a long, broken road ahead of us, but we're going to take it."

Dad cupped Mom's hand in his. "This time, we're not traveling alone." And he began to pray.

Why did there have to be a blizzard, today of all days?

Her wedding slash vow-renewal day.

Ronnie tugged the guest room curtains shut and plopped down on the bed. Fifteen minutes until the renewal, and the storm raged harder than ever. Why even bother dressing up if guests, the few they'd invited, couldn't attend?

There she went again, acting like a spoiled-rotten diva. God had been doing a good work in her, but she was still a work in progress.

She got up and aimed for the closet where the red cocktail dress awaited her—the perfect Christmas dress. Even if it was just her, Gavin, Evie, and Mom and Dad, that was all they needed to create a memorable day. Especially if Mom and Dad continued to get along.

Maybe sometime soon her parents would have their own vow renewal ceremony. Ronnie wouldn't let a blizzard stop her from witnessing that.

Knock. Knock. Knock.

Ronnie hurried to the door and yelled through it, "If

that's Gavin, you need to go away. I'll see you in about fifteen minutes."

"It's Mom."

Oh, perfect. Ronnie flung open the door and gasped. Mom looked stunning in her pale green lace-covered sheath that stopped just above her knees, showing off her shapely legs. Loose curls framed her face.

Ronnie waved her mom in. "Dad won't be able to take his eyes off you."

"That's the goal." Mom even blushed. Yes! The two were well on their way back to marital bliss.

"Well, my goal is to see Gavin's eyes bug out." She hurried to her closet and retrieved her dress. "Would you mind giving me a hand?"

"I can't believe you're not ready yet." Mom unzipped the dress as Ronnie pulled off her nightgown.

"I was too busy pouting." She nodded to the window.

Mom waved her hand. "It'll be a lovely ceremony, with or without more guests. The true focus is on your marriage."

Spoken by someone with years of experience in both the good and the bad. Advice Ronnie wouldn't take for granted.

Mom helped her into her dress, zipped up the back, and then helped with the final hair and makeup touches.

She looked good, even if she did say so herself. She couldn't wait to see Gavin's reaction.

"Ready?" Mom stepped back, had Ronnie turn in a circle, then nodded, blinking away a tear. She inhaled and breathed out. "I can't believe my baby girl's getting married."

"I'm already married."

"Yes, but this time." Mom nodded. "This time it's for real. This time it's because you're in love with the man, not the fluff attached to him."

"I am," she said softly. Deeply in love.

"I'll let the men know." Mom opened the bedroom door. "When you hear music, that's your cue." She stepped out and disappeared down the hallway.

Ronnie took in another deep breath and listened. The music wouldn't be live like they'd planned. Kyle and his wife, Trip, were supposed to play and sing. Others thought it strange she'd invite her ex to her vow renewal, but they were family, linked through Evie. The adults needed to set the example of how to get along.

Keyboard music drifted toward her, along with the strum of a guitar. It sure didn't sound piped-in—it sounded live. Though, Gavin's sound system was probably the best money could buy.

She felt in her dress pocket for a tissue. It was there, just in case. Then she followed the music down the hallway, to the top of the curved stairway leading to the home's grand entry where the ceremony would be held.

She looked down and had to blink to stop the tears. Somehow, with the storm raging outside, guests had arrived. Kyle and Trip. Her boss, Hannah. A couple of Gavin's colleagues.

How?

Even Amy and Geoffrey, the couple they'd met at Lake

Itasca, were in attendance.

Ronnie focused on Gavin, who had the biggest grin on his face, then her dad who appeared teary-eyed.

"Mama pretty." Evie broke away from Mom and ran toward the stairs.

"Come here, baby girl." Ronnie walked down the garland-wrapped staircase as Kyle played "Still, Still, Still" on the keyboard.

Evie ran to her and lifted her hands, but Ronnie shook her head. "You're a big girl now. You can walk." She took her daughter's hand, and together they walked down the staircase, then past three rows of seats. She tried to release Evie's hand when they reached Gavin, but her daughter held firm.

Well, then, that was okay. Gavin was marrying Ronnie, but Evie was part of the package deal.

Holding both Gavin's and Evie's hands, she whispered to Gavin, "How are all these people here?"

He shrugged. "Well, Amy and Geoffrey rode in on snowmobile this morning. The rest stayed with very kind neighbors, who opened their homes last night before the storm."

Very kind, indeed. Ronnie mentally logged a note to send the neighbors a "Thank you."

Dad said a few words—the plan was to keep the ceremony short and sweet so they could enjoy the reception afterwards. He asked if they'd reaffirm their love for each other, and they each said, "I will." Then Kyle and Trip sang a duet of Matthew West's "When I Say I Do."

The important part of the ceremony was the vows they'd written for each other, which she didn't know how she'd make it through.

Good thing Gavin was going first.

He knelt and said to Evie, "May I hold your Mommy's hand?"

"Okay." Evie let go and ran to Dada Kyle.

Then Gavin took both her hands in his. He looked in her eyes so deeply, she swore he could see right to her soul, and it stole her breath away.

"My dearest Veronica." He raised a hand to his lips and kissed it. "My love for you caught me completely off guard. You took this socially awkward, confirmed bachelor and opened my heart, helped me break from my self-built shell. Watching you grow in faith over these past several months has deepened my own faith. I can't wait to see what plans God has for our family."

He looked over at Evie. "I look forward to being Evie's step Dada. Praying for her, being a firsthand witness to her faith story." Then back at Ronnie. "I promise to love you, sacrificially, as Jesus modeled. As we've seen, life will take us down rough paths, but I promise to walk with you and hold your hand on those paths. With God at the center of our marriage, with Him strengthening our love, we'll hold strong. I love your dearly, Veronica Joy."

A rogue tear escaped her eye, but she let it fall as she prayed for help to make it through. Thank goodness for streak-free mascara.

She squeezed Gavin's hands. "What you saw in me, this

spoiled drama queen, I'll never know. But I do know that without you, I never would have grown. I never would have examined my faith and found it lacking. I never would have learned that following Jesus is much more than attending church services and singing a few songs. From the moment I met you, you demonstrated the truth about love, and you've loved someone not deserving. I promise to love you back with all my being. I promise to keep God at our center. And I look forward to holding your hand on all those rutty paths we'll be walking. I love you more than I dreamed possible. Thank you for loving me and Evie. You are the best part of our lives."

Dad said a few more words that Ronnie didn't comprehend. They exchanged rings. Dad said something else, followed by, "It's my honor and privilege to reaffirm your marriage. Celebrate this renewal with a kiss."

Gavin leaned in for a chaste kiss, but then released her hands and wrapped his arms around her back, taking the kiss deeper than she expected.

Not that she was complaining.

"Me too, kiss."

They broke apart and looked down at Evie, her arms raised. Gavin quickly scooped her up and looked her in the eye. "I affirm that I will be the best dada possible for you, Evelyn, that I will love you always."

She pressed her pudgy hands against his cheeks and gave him a kiss on the lips. "I wuv you, too, Dada Gabin."

*"If you abide in my word,
you are truly my disciples,
and you will know the truth,
and the truth will set you free."*
John 8:31-32

Dear Reader,

*After I typed "The End" to **Song of Mercy**, I knew that Ronnie, a secondary character, needed her own redemption story. I loved watching her grow in her faith once she learned that Jesus is The Truth!*

Unfortunately, Ronnie's story is played out too often in churches that crave popularity over staying true to the Gospels. If you want to know who Jesus is, I've included the Seven "I Am" Statements and 50 Names of Jesus to give you a glimpse into who He is. The best way to know Him better is through reading the Word and remaining in prayer.

You'll find further inspiration and encouragement on The Potter's House Books Website, (www.pottershousebooks.com) and by reading the other books in the series. Read them all and be encouraged and uplifted!

In Him,

Brenda

Seven "I Am" Statements

"I am the bread of life;
whoever comes to me shall not hunger,
and whoever believes in me shall never thirst."
John 6:35

"I am the light of the world.
Whoever follows me will not walk in darkness,
but will have the light of life."
John 8:12

"Truly, truly, I say to you, I am the door of the sheep...
I am the door.
If anyone enters by me, he will be saved and will go in
and out and find pasture."
John 10:7, 9

"I am the resurrection and the life.
Whoever believes in me, though he die, yet shall he live..."
John 11:25

"I am the good shepherd.
The good shepherd lays down his life for the sheep...
I am the good shepherd.
I know my own and my own know me..."
John 10:11, 14

"I am the way, and the truth, and the life.
No one comes to the Father except through me."
John 14:6

"I am the true vine, and my Father is the vinedresser...
I am the vine; you are the branches.
Whoever abides in me and I in him,
he it is that bears much fruit,
for apart from me you can do nothing."
John 15:1, 5

50 Names of Jesus

(Not an exhaustive list)

Almighty One, Alpha and Omega, Advocate,
Author and Perfector of Our Faith, Authority,
Bread of Life, Beloved Son of God, Bridegroom,
Bright Morning Star, Chief Cornerstone, Deliverer,
Faithful and True, Good Shepherd, Great High Priest,
Good Shepherd, Holy One, Horn of Salvation,
I Am,
Immanuel, Judge, King of Kings, Lamb of God,
Light of the World, Lion of the Tribe of Judah, Lord of All,
Mediator, Messiah, Mighty One, One Who Sets Free,
Our Hope, Peace, Prophet, Redeemer, Risen Lord, Rock,
Savior, Servant, Son of Man, Supreme Creator Over All,
The Door, The Resurrection and the Life, The Truth,
The Way, The Word, True Vine, Victorious One,
Wonderful Counselor, Mighty God, Everlasting Father,
Prince of Peace

Acknowledgements

I can't believe I've been writing with The Potter's House Books for two years! What an honor it's been writing alongside so many gifted authors! Thank you for welcoming me.

Thanks also goes to:

My Readers ~ You are the reason I keep writing.

My Book Booster Team ~ for continuing to spread the word about my books.

Lesley Ann McDaniel ~ for polishing my stories.

Gayle Balster ~ for always being my first-read guinea pig.

Sarah, Bryan, and Brandon ~ for your continuous support!

My husband, Marvin ~ for being my helpmate and number one encourager this entire crazy year.

And thank you, Jesus. You are The Way, The Truth, and The Life. I hope my stories offer a reflection of who you are.

Potter's House Books

by Brenda S. Anderson

Hands of Grace #4 of Series 2
Song of Mercy #12 of Series 2
Season of Hope #20 of Series 2

Long Way Home #4
Place Called Home#11
Home Another Way #18

FIND ALL THE POTTER'S HOUSE BOOKS AT

www.PottersHouseBooks.com.

Other Books

BY BRENDA S. ANDERSON

www.BrendaAndersonBooks.com/books

THE MOSAIC COLLECTION

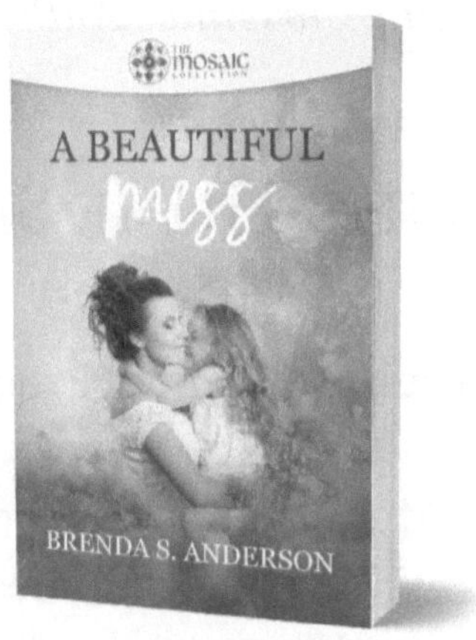

A BEAUTIFUL MESS

"Anderson delivers an impactful story about the power of faith within flawed, complicated people. . . . Readers who enjoy the work of Karen Kingsbury should check this out."
—**Publishers Weekly**/Booklife

A BEAUTIFUL CHRIST-MESS
A Mosaic Collection Short Story

Mosaic Collection Anthologies

Hope is Born
(A Mosaic Christmas Anthology)
Before Summer's End
A Star Will Rise
(A Mosaic Christmas Anthology II)

Coming Home Series

Pieces of Granite (Prequel)
Chain of Mercy
Memory Box Secrets
Hungry for Home
Coming Home (a short story)
A Christmas Homecoming (a short story)

Where the Heart Is Series

Risking Love
Capturing Beauty
Planting Hope

About the Author

 **Brenda S. Anderson** writes gritty and authentic, life-affirming fiction. She is a member of the American Christian Fiction Writers, and is Past-President of the ACFW Minnesota chapter, MN-NICE. When not reading or writing, she enjoys music, theater, roller coasters, and baseball, and she loves watching movies with her family. She resides in the Minneapolis, Minnesota area with her husband of 30-plus years and one sassy cat.

Let's Connect

Visit Brenda online at www.BrendaAndersonBooks.com and on Facebook, Goodreads, Instagram, and BookBub.

For news and encouragement about upcoming books, contests, giveaways, and other activities, sign up for Brenda's bi-monthly newsletter.

If you enjoyed *Season of Hope*, please consider leaving a review. Your words bring hope and encouragement to the author, as well as other readers.